Voices in the Waiting Room

Mayank Gupta is a writer who observes life from the edges, diving into the messy spaces where our thoughts splinter and our identities get wobbly. His stories explore the often ignored shadows of human experience, capturing those moments that lie just beneath the surface.

As a triple board-certified psychiatrist, Mayank's fiction is deeply influenced by his years of practice in places such as Mumbai, London and New York, where he's witnessed the complexities of identity and the human psyche. Rather than providing neat conclusions or redemption, his work invites readers to embrace uncertainty, to feel the dissonance of life and to navigate the intricate landscapes of consciousness. In Mayank's stories, you won't find tidy endings—just the raw beauty of what is left when we peel back the layers of our façades.

Voices in the Waiting Room

Mayank Gupta

Published by
Rupa Publications India Pvt. Ltd 2025
7/16, Ansari Road, Daryaganj
New Delhi 110002

Sales centres:
Bengaluru Chennai Hyderabad
Jaipur Kathmandu Kolkata
Mumbai Prayagraj

Copyright © Mayank Gupta 2025

This is a work of fiction. Names, characters, places and incidents are either the product of the author's imagination or are used fictitiously and any resemblance to any actual person, living or dead, events or locales is entirely coincidental.

All rights reserved.
No part of this publication may be reproduced, transmitted or stored in a retrieval system, in any form or by any means, electronic, mechanical, photocopying, recording or otherwise, without the prior permission of the publisher.

P-ISBN: 978-93-7003-218-7
E-ISBN: 978-93-7003-706-9

First impression 2025

10 9 8 7 6 5 4 3 2 1

The moral right of the author has been asserted.

Printed in India

This book is sold subject to the condition that it shall not, by way of trade or otherwise, be lent, resold, hired out or otherwise circulated, without the publisher's prior consent, in any form of binding or cover other than that in which it is published.

Dedicated to every street child.

May this book honour your resilience and fortitude in the face of adversity.

May it stand as a testament to your right to be seen, heard and treated with dignity, even if its contents unsettle or challenge the readers.

Contents

Author's Note		ix
1	Unchanging	1
2	Bourgeoisie	8
3	Dreaming	13
4	Running on the Edge	26
5	Aesthetics	31
6	Reunion	36
7	Tour de Force	46
8	Unfinished Juxtaposition	51
9	Siberian Cranes	67
10	Tolerating Ambiguity	75
11	JEDI Stands For Justice, Equity, Diversity and Inclusion	78
12	Status Quo	87
13	Reconciling with the Past	94
14	Identity Crisis	106
15	Caring for Oligarchs	116

16	Education without Wisdom	123
17	Losing Chumships	126
18	Can't Remember but Can't Forget	135
19	Privilege	141
20	Hate Nobody	144
21	Transcending Bystander Effect	149
22	Indoctrination: The Pathway to a Curated Life	151
23	Humans: Truth-Telling Machines	159
24	Becoming	163
25	Omnipotence in Bursting Mode	166
26	The Right to Make Mistakes	171
27	Redemption	175
28	Integrity or Despair	178
29	The Last Sacrifice	181
30	The Silence between Words	183
Epilogue		189
Acknowledgements		196

Author's Note

The inspiration for writing this book stemmed from my decision to carefully observe and unapologetically question everything. Over more than two decades of introspection, I have scrutinized the prevailing disparities and biases of our time. While the right to health is indisputably fundamental, it is all too often overshadowed by various hegemonies, systemic oppression and bigotry. It's crucial to recognize that those who perpetrate these injustices are not immune to their consequences—their actions ultimately affect both themselves and their loved ones.

This book offers a bold critique, intended to provoke discomfort and foster awareness. My aim is to stimulate critical thinking and provide an alternative perspective on how our society addresses these issues. Despite the discomfort it may evoke, I remain optimistic, drawing inspiration from the virtues of the new generation. I believe that by sharing experiences and stories, I have helped illuminate something paramount to our shared existence. Thus, by utilizing art as a universal language, I seek to introduce complex issues and ideas into public discourse.

Moreover, this book explores the intersection of societal conventions and health, underscoring their bidirectional interconnectedness with myriad hidden factors, including but not limited to institutions, systems and oppression. By confronting uncomfortable contradictions, I challenge readers to grapple with ambivalence and take the risk of thinking deeply.

—Mayank Gupta

1
Unchanging

Dr Silva's House

'I swear by Apollo Physician and Asclepius and Hygieia and Panacea and all the gods and goddesses, making them my witnesses, that I will fulfil according to my ability and judgement this oath and this covenant…'

The words blurred as Dr Silva lost focus, her gaze slipping from the brass plate she kept at her bedside. Not that she needed to read the words—they were etched into her memory as firmly as if carved in stone. Several nights a week, unable to sleep, she would sit up in bed, clutching the cold metal plate, staring at it for hours. She would murmur the Oath of Hippocrates over and over, chuckling at the bitter irony. Reciting it gave her a sense of fidelity—to the oath, to her patients and, in a way, to herself.

The brass plate, roughly the size of a large saucer, bore the Oath in an elegant cursive font. It had been a gift from the then Finance Minister of Mexico, also infamously known as 'The Most Arrogant Man in Mexico'. Years earlier, Dr Silva had saved his life, treating him for stage III oesophageal cancer; the politician had wept with gratitude while thanking her.

Rachel, her apprentice, had been impressed. 'That man has probably never even thanked his own mother,' she had remarked one afternoon.

Among many other things, Dr Silva had a knack for identifying narcissists. She had known the moment she met the minister that he was a textbook case. It is a strange thing: death is the ultimate truth, one we all choose to ignore. It cannot be avoided, no matter how fiercely we cling to life. Yet the most arrogant often seem the most desperate to live forever. Perhaps it was the weight of their unlived lives.

Setting the plate aside on her bedside table, she glanced at the digital clock. It was 4.45 a.m. Time to begin her day. She got up, dressed quickly and went out for her morning run. She promised herself she'd focus solely on the rhythmic thud of her feet against the asphalt and the steady cadence of her breath. Performing tasks with complete presence, she believed, was a form of meditation few people practised. It was as difficult as sitting still and clearing one's mind of all thoughts.

The tranquillity did not last long. Her thoughts re-emerged, but she was unsure what to do with them.

By the time she returned, it was 6.30 a.m. As she thought about the day ahead, her assistant called, as if on cue.

'Good morning, Dr Silva,' Rachel's voice boomed through the phone.

'First up on your schedule is a visit to the patient in Room 74 at 8 a.m. She's showing a considerable positive response to the new treatment algorithm you put her on yesterday. Then, Jake Shawn has booked the 11.30 a.m. appointment—he wants a consult for a mandibular enhancement procedure. He's the Pesky Bandits star, you know? Like, the greatest football quarterback! I am a big fan. Maybe I can ask for his autograph?' Rachel's effervescent tone rattled off the day's agenda. 'Oh! Also, there's a super important fundraiser lunch at City Hall at 1 p.m. The mayor has already called twice, specifically requesting your presence. I'll have an afternoon dress laid out in your office, along with your makeup box and your speech. Lastly, you have got two candidates for the 5 p.m. slot: Joe Flash—the baseball player—wants a rhinoplasty; apparently, he has broken his nose again. The other is some hotshot British sitcom star. He has no idea what he wants, though. Do you have any preferences?'

Dr Silva's irritation bubbled just beneath the surface. 'I already have a 5 p.m. scheduled, Rachel,' she sighed.

Dr Silva knew precisely who her preference was, and it wasn't either of these two. A certain A-list actor from India, Mr Kapoor, was en route for the evening appointment. At that moment, he was on a flight with his entourage of managers, security personnel, a dietician, chefs and whatnot—clutching a glowing personal recommendation, which had come in the form of a late-night international phone call the previous week from a key lawmaker she had known for a decade.

'Sorry, Doctor. I completely forgot about that. The actor is from India, right?' Rachel asked.

'Yes.'

'I am surprised you agreed to see him on such short notice. You never make allowances for anyone. May I—?'

'No, you may not ask why,' Dr Silva cut Rachel short. 'I will tell you if I need to. And from now on, handle all the calls with Shukla, no matter what. Now, if that is all, I will see you at the hospital.'

Dr Silva ended the call without waiting for Rachel's response. She knew it was rude but irritation prickled at her skin—the kind that came from having to compromise her principles. The fact that it was necessary for achieving her dream didn't soothe her much now.

The politician had tried to reach her several times, but all her calls were filtered through Rachel. Dr Silva owned a mobile phone but rarely used it. Only Rachel had her personal number and was allowed to call between 6.30 and 7 a.m. No one needed to know about her non-existent personal life, not even Rachel. The moment Rachel had mentioned Shukla, she knew she'd have to bend her rules—even before she took that immoral politician's call.

'Madam-ji, this is a high-profile and urgent case. You watch Indian movies, don't you? You know how it is in the film industry. We want to see the same actor but with a different heroine every time. Mr Kapoor is turning 49 next month, and he has three movies lined up. One of them is a war film—he's playing a young, patriotic soldier. His performance needs to evoke pathos and nationalism, and for that, we must take care of his saggy cheeks. Certainly, you can do something about it,' Shukla had said, his voice oozing sly charm.

'I went through the file you sent me,' Dr Silva had replied. 'My suggestion would be a European higher cheekbone prosthetic procedure—it would take at least 10 years off his face. But you have to understand that it'd take me months to fit him into my schedule. I can recommend an excellent facility and plastic surgeon, though; Mr Kapoor will have no complaints.'

The Indian film industry's obsession with European features is almost laughable, especially given that Kapoor's upcoming film is meant to be a patriotic tribute. No wonder so many popular actresses have relocated from the West to the East—they had to keep up with the standards. Does it smell like hypocrisy? Or am I just overthinking? she had thought.

'Because you are the best, madam-ji,' Shukla had wheedled. 'Consider it a service to foreign relations,' he had added with a chuckle.

'Mr Shukla, is there any development on what we last discussed?' Dr Silva had asked, seeking a morsel of hope.

'Madam-ji, rest assured, I'm trying my best; India is a complex country—these things take time,' Shukla had replied, evasive.

For the first time in her entire medical career, Dr Anita Silva had agreed to see a patient on a recommendation—something she'd never done before, no matter the referrer. But this was different.

There was a hazy longing gnawing at her—a sense of being incomplete, as though she were staring into a smoke screen, unable to see what lay beyond. Something was missing, but she couldn't define it. There was something she couldn't remember but also couldn't forget, and it haunted her every night. Her sleep was riddled with fuzzy, disjointed dreams—sometimes terrifying but always fleeting and impossible to grasp. She often woke up in despair, trying to hold on to blurry scenes that flashed by in fragmented bursts and left her clawing at elusive details that slipped through her fingers like sand, robbing her of peace.

In her waking hours, Dr Silva had tried to pry open these dreams, poking at them like a scab that refused to heal. But when she couldn't find the answers in her mind, she sought peace elsewhere. Beyond her unwavering commitment to excellence in cancer research, surgery and development of complex treatment algorithms, she found herself drawn to art galleries. It was art that brought her solace and inspiration.

Her home was more than a residence—it was a private gallery, her sanctuary, filled with paintings, sculptures and eclectic artefacts from various cultures. Her collection was vast and highly sophisticated, featuring rare, expensive pieces that reflected her refined taste and passion.

She was renowned throughout the city and beyond as one of the largest curators and collectors of rare art. Her distinct interest in unusual and extraordinary forms set her apart. She always found a way to source and acquire pieces that captivated her. Her home was a testament to her artistic spirit and her ability to connect deeply with the beauty and meaning art brought to her life. It was the one thing that filled the hollowness her dreams left behind. But it was also this vested interest that had unintentionally brought her face to face with what she had been running from.

About a year ago, a patient referred by Shukla had gifted her some ethnic artefacts as a token of gratitude. Among them was a set of bangles adorned with an unusual art form. The moment she laid eyes on it, something inside her had lurched. It had triggered an intense emotional reckoning, leaving her shaken.

The bangles had become an obsession—she had to trace the origin of the art form. Getting that piece of information felt like finally finding a missing piece of a puzzle. It was no longer about the art—it was about understanding herself and unlocking her dreams.

And so, she had gritted her teeth and obliged. Deciding that it was the first and last time she'd let herself get swayed, Dr Silva justified this break in character as necessary for the greater good.

As she prepared to leave for the hospital, her eyes fell on the brass plate and the Oath of Hippocrates stared back at her.

2
Bourgeoisie

Office of the Director of Education
Northbridge General Hospital

'A mouse!' Dr Gray was having a flashback to high school, when a bully had called him a mouse. 'Yes, that is what you look like—a mouse.'

Sitting across from the dean in his office, Dr Gray had spent the better part of the last hour trying to figure out which creature the man resembled.

The dean had been droning on in his squeaky voice about how the institute always conducted a fair interview process and that candidates were selected purely on merit.

'Are you aware of the term "White Men's Club", Dr Hawker?' Dr Gray interrupted at last. 'I wouldn't be surprised if you weren't. Even I wasn't aware of it until last morning. Some journalist with far too much time on his hands coined it in an article published in yesterday's edition of *The Mail*. In case you missed it, let me give you the gist.'

Dr Hawker's brow furrowed.

The article claims our higher education system—

particularly the medical entrance interview process—is heavily biased. The selected candidates, it argues, are as white as a sheet. It alleges not only that the children of wealthy, established doctors are favoured, but also that there's racial and ethnic profiling at play.'

Dr Hawker's eyes widened in disbelief, his expression shifting to one of growing concern.

'These claims are backed by statistics, Dr Hawker,' the director continued. 'The journalist compiled data from the past 10 years of medical entrance interviews, as well as major Ivy League interviews, and crunched the numbers. The result? 87 per cent of the candidates are White, and 72 per cent come from alumni families—mostly siblings or children. This biased selection process is what he termed the "White Men's Club". A really catchy term, don't you think so, Dr Hawker?' Dr Gray concluded, staring at the dean with pity.

'I thought that was only limited to fraternities and sororities… I…I didn't realize it was systemic,' Dr Hawker stammered, breaking into a cold sweat. His short arms flailed, as if trying to push the information away.

Suddenly, he slammed his fist on the table. 'This is nonsense! I can't believe this is still happening. How can we deny someone who truly deserves it? How can we hand the same position to someone else based on these ridiculous pretexts? It doesn't make sense—none of it! Do you have any idea what this will do to the quality of education? To the quality of healthcare? You think we can afford to let this happen? The whole system is going to collapse!' Hawker's voice shook in frustration, the words spilling out like a dam breaking, his indignation cutting through the room like a blade.

Dr Gray leaned back, arms crossed, eyes steady. 'Danny,' he began, his voice low but firm. 'I've known you since med school. I watched you climb your way to the top. But don't make me say things I've held back for years. You want to call me a victim? Fine. I *am* a victim—of the very privilege you refuse to acknowledge. Do you even understand what it means to be pushed to the margins? To exist in a system that only serves the mainstream? Every great society, every just civilization, protects those on the edges. And you? You've become the kind of bigot I should've confronted long ago. But I didn't. And for that, I blame myself.'

The room froze as Dr Gray's words hung heavy in the air.

Hawker's face flushed a livid shade of red. 'Shut up,' he hissed, his voice trembling with fury. 'Just shut up, you idiot! You've always been a loser, sitting in the corner, never saying a word. And now—*now* you think you can sit there and accuse me? Do you have any idea what I've sacrificed? What I've worked for my entire life? You're trying to take it all away from me, and it's insane—it's completely insane!' His voice cracked, then abruptly faltered.

Silence. Heavy and suffocating, it filled the room like the aftermath of a storm leaving destruction in its wake.

Dr Hawker lowered his gaze, his breath unsteady. 'I... I don't know what I'm saying,' he muttered, almost to himself. His shoulders sagged. He glanced at Dr Gray, his eyes clouded with something that looked like shame. 'I'm sorry. I... This is all so rattling. I think... I think I'm losing it because...because I see what's happening to you. And it's happening to my son, too.' He rubbed his temple, his voice breaking. 'Let me just...take a moment. I'm sorry.'

Dr Gray sighed. 'You must understand, this has caused quite a stir in Congress. As Director of Education, it falls on my shoulders to not only investigate these outrageous claims but also make sure the opposition cannot use them as an excuse to undo all the good work we've done here so far.

'Listen to me, Danny, and listen very carefully, for I'm only going to say this once: stop with this elitist behaviour right now. This year, instead of relying on recommendations from your colleagues, focus on recruiting trainees from diverse ethnic, racial and cultural backgrounds... Even North Koreans, if we can convince them to go back as American spies, maybe,' Dr Gray chuckled dryly at his own joke.

'A political think tank analysed why the great Roman, Greek, British and Ottoman empires collapsed, and we don't want to make the same mistake,' he added.

'Why did they collapse?' Dr Hawker asked, his voice barely a whisper.

'Because when power lies with a few, it leads to mutiny; the people left behind—the ones marginalized by systemic oppression—create deep fissures in society, eventually leading to its collapse. Now you may go, sir. Thank you for coming,' Dr Gray replied.

Without another word, Dr Hawker scuttled out of the room as fast as he could—almost scampering.

Dr Gray chuckled. *The only good thing to come out of all this is that this year, the selections will be more deserving*, he thought, amused by how well the meeting had gone.

∞

3

Dreaming

Mid-air, Chicago to New York

'India?'

'Huh, what?'

If there was one thing Ankit hated more than early morning flights, it was chatty co-passengers. Squinting slightly, he turned to the old man sitting next to him. At first glance, it was hard to tell, but he seemed Indian too. His salt-and-pepper beard was neatly trimmed and he carried a faint hint of sandalwood; his eyes, distant and wistful, seemed to hold stories untold.

'Are you from North India?' the man asked again, his American accent surprisingly perfect.

'Uh, no, sir, I'm from Palamgarh. How did you know I am Indian?'

The old man chuckled. 'Well, I knew you were Indian the moment I saw you, son. That belly of yours is definitely irrigated by ghee, and your hair is irrigated by oil. There's no mistaking the Indianness in you.' He extended his hand. 'Anyway, I'm Dr Ravi Jindal; nice to meet you.'

'Dr Ankit; nice to meet you too, sir.'

A little irritated by the unsolicited conversation, Ankit

signalled to the flight attendant. 'Can I get a coffee?' he asked, his voice sharper than intended.

'What would you like, sir?' the attendant replied, unfazed, her tone calm and polite.

'Something strong,' Ankit requested, rubbing his temple.

She paused, thinking. 'Why don't you try an Americano?'

'What's that?' Ankit asked, the exhaustion in his voice giving way to mild curiosity.

Before the attendant could answer, Dr Jindal leaned in with a wry smile. 'That's where you get 400 milligrams of caffeine in one go,' he said, the faintest glimmer of amusement in his eyes.

Ankit blinked, surprised. 'Really? That's more than the recommended daily intake.'

Dr Jindal chuckled and shrugged. 'That's the American way.'

The flight attendant smirked at their exchange before disappearing to fetch the coffee. Moments later, she returned with a steaming cup of Americano and set it gently on Ankit's tray table.

He nodded his thanks and took a long sip. The bold bitterness jolted him awake almost immediately. He finished the cup quickly, hoping the caffeine would kick-start his brain, sharpening his focus for the conversation he now felt inclined to have. Ankit wasn't usually one for mid-flight chatter, but there was something promising about Dr Jindal. The man seemed like someone who might have valuable insights—insights that could prove helpful for the important meeting Ankit was heading towards.

'Where are you headed, Ankit?' Dr Jindal's voice broke through Ankit's thoughts.

'I'm going to Northbridge General Hospital, sir. That's my interview centre for the postgraduate residency programme,' Ankit said.

'Oh, what a coincidence!' Dr Jindal's face lit up. 'I work there as an anaesthesiologist, and had come to Chicago for a conference. Postgraduate residency, huh? I assume you've cleared your clinical skills examination, then?'

'Yes, sir, I have. I applied for the surgical oncology residency, headed by Dr Silva, and my application was selected. Today is the interview.'

'All the very best to you, son. Dr Silva is a good acquaintance of mine. There's no one else I can think of who is board-certified in both plastic surgery and surgical oncology.' Dr Jindal paused, then turned to his side to give Ankit his full attention. 'Where are you staying, by the way?'

Ankit hesitated slightly, unsure why Dr Jindal was interested in this piece of information. 'Currently, I have been provided accommodation by the hospital management at Economy Lodge; I will be staying there for a few days, sir.'

'And how do you plan to spend this time? You'll be done with the interview today, I suppose?' Dr Jindal pressed on.

'No,' Ankit replied, sensing a string of personal questions coming his way. 'I have applied for residency at a few other institutions. I'll be spending most of my time here interviewing at all of them. But I do plan to do a bit of sightseeing and accommodation hunting. In case I get selected, I won't have much time later to look for a place to live, so I'd rather take care of that beforehand.'

He then thought of taking advantage of the, hopefully, well-meaning doctor. 'Can you suggest any ethnic-friendly neighbourhoods here?' Ankit asked.

For some reason, the question brought a smile to Dr Jindal's face. 'Ethnic-friendly?' he repeated, raising an eyebrow. 'I've lived here for 33 years now, and I'd rather live in a "friendly" neighbourhood than an "ethnic-friendly" one—if there even is such a thing.'

He let out a dry chuckle before continuing. 'It might come as a bit of a surprise, but if you think people here are better than back home, you're in for a big shock, son. Just like we have a social divide in India, there's one here too. The only difference is that instead of caste and religion, the divide is based on class and race.'

Don't get me wrong,' Dr Jindal added. 'As physicians, those who know us value and respect us. But when we are on the streets, we are just coloured guys. Have you heard of supremacist cults? If not, I suggest you read about them.' He paused, then reached into his coat pocket and handed Ankit a business card. 'Anyway, here—this is my card; keep it. Drop me a text as soon as you are done with the interview; I may be able to help you out with accommodation.'

Ankit pocketed the card and thanked Dr Jindal.

At the baggage carousel, as Ankit waited for his bags, he looked at his watch and felt his stomach tighten. 8.53 a.m. At this pace, he was going to be late.

Collecting his bags, he quickly left the airport and boarded a local shuttle to reach the main bus stop.

It's the last stop, and I guess the bus is running late today, Ankit thought, peering out the window at the sluggish traffic. When the shuttle finally pulled in, he hopped on to bus number 101. He tapped his foot impatiently, silently urging the bus to move faster.

The vehicle groaned and rattled like an old man with lung disease, shuddering at every turn. When it finally came to a wheezing halt at Northbridge General Hospital, it was 9.45 a.m.

Ankit dashed towards the entrance, mentally calculating that he had exactly 15 minutes to freshen up and report for the interview at Wing C.

One look at the hospital campus told him finding Wing C was going to be a real pain.

The sprawling campus was dotted with Victorian-style buildings and modern additions, creating a peculiar but striking blend of historical and contemporary architecture. The road leading to the entrance was lined with pine trees, standing tall and proud on either side. The expansive, lush green grounds stretched out before him, buzzing with activity—students deep in conversation or sulking in the sun, visitors milling about or patients in recovery strolling for fresh air.

Fifteen minutes later, Ankit reached Wing C and joined the long queue of doctors waiting for their turn, panting and trying to catch his breath. *Sixty per cent of the people standing in this line seem to be South Asians*, he thought, scanning the faces.

Dressed in a suit complete with a matching tie, Ankit stood out awkwardly from the rest, most of whom were casually dressed in denim and loose shirts. It was then that he realized how different interviews there were from the ones back in India. The atmosphere was laid-back and the candidates looked relaxed, while he was overdressed, tense and drenched in sweat.

A familiar wave of anxiety washed over him, his heart pounding in his chest as his breath quickened. Cold sweat prickled his skin and his hands felt distant, unreal, as if they did not belong to him. That strange sensation of derealization crept in—the unsettling feeling of being slightly unmoored from reality.

He clenched his fists, trying to ground himself. He recalled what his friend had told him. 'It is not always about popping a beta blocker like propranolol to calm your heart. Sometimes, it is about taking deep, deliberate breaths, slow and sharp. That is how you take control.'

Ankit inhaled deeply, filling his lungs with air, forcing his mind to focus on the rhythmic thud of his heartbeat. *What do I have to lose?* he thought. But he knew the answer. *Everything.*

The stakes were monumental, and the knowledge of that gnawed at him as he tried to rationalize his way through it. The pit in his stomach grumbled, his hands felt damp; his gaze wandered to the other candidates, their confidence radiating like an aura he could not ignore. He could not help but compare, feeling as though, objectively, they were better than him.

But then came another thought—sharper and more critical. *We humans are funny creatures*, he mused. *We see ourselves subjectively and others objectively; but shouldn't it be the other way around? Shouldn't we judge ourselves with cold logic and see others with compassion and nuance?* The realization struck him, yet it did not erase the self-doubt swirling within his mind.

He wiped his clammy palms on his trousers, willing himself to stay grounded. As his turn inched closer, his thoughts drifted to the panel waiting beyond the door. Would they judge him on his words, his ideas, his body language? Would they be swayed by his charisma or would they remain trapped in their own hidden biases? There was no way of knowing. And that was what unsettled him the most—the entire process felt far too human, far too flawed. How could anyone objectively assess someone's worth in the span of a single conversation?

But there were no escapes, no shortcuts. After years of dedication to a profession he loved, this was the system he had to navigate. He straightened his back, drew in a deep breath and prepared himself to step into the unknown. Whatever lay beyond that door, he would face it head-on—even if his thoughts were still tangled in a thousand threads of uncertainty.

When his turn finally came, he was ushered into the interview room—a repurposed old OPD. It reeked of disinfectants, stale air and the faint, morbid scent of ageing and death.

Why would they use an OPD for the interview? Ankit thought as he walked in. *Maybe it is a tactic to overwhelm candidates.*

The room was sterile and cold. A long table stood in the centre, with seven chairs on one side for the panel and a single chair on the other side for the interviewee.

As Ankit scanned the room, his mind was a whirlwind of thoughts. *How,* he wondered, *could a panel of strangers— several of them, no less—ever hope to grasp the depth of his subjectivity, the layers of his unique perspective?*

His curriculum vitae already laid out the facts, the measurable achievements, the so-called objectivity of his career. But how could he convey the intangible—the charisma, the human essence, the ability to connect, to express, to inspire? Those traits were the true markers of success, weren't they? And yet, here he was, trying to reduce his humanity into polished sentences and sterile professionalism for people who held his fate in their hands.

The interview panel consisted of seven doctors, including the dean, Dr Hawker, he noted.

'Good morning, gentlemen,' Ankit greeted them.

'Good morning, Dr Ankit; please have a seat,' one of the doctors said.

The five-second walk from the door to the chair felt like a slow-motion montage—a blitz of whispered prayers to every god he could remember, interspersed with flashbacks of late-night poring over books. Hours upon hours of labour, book after book crammed into the brain for this moment. *All of it now boils down to how I perform today*, he thought.

How much he could remember was going to decide his future.

'Tell us something about yourself, Dr Ankit.'

Umm, what? Ankit's thoughts stuttered. *Now that's one weird first question.*

He had expected technical queries, not a personality assessment. Back in India, medical interviews were all about obscure diagnoses and rapid-fire recall. The culture there rarely valued individuality—it was about proving how much you knew, not who you were. Many times, success lay in the fine line between humility and humiliation.

His hands were slightly shaky as he responded, 'Sir, my name is Ankit, and I come from a small town called Palamgarh in India. I did my medical schooling at St George Medical College, Jaigarh.'

One of the doctors raised an eyebrow and leaned forward slightly. 'We don't want to know your academic details, Ankit; we can find that out from your resume. We want to know who you are as a person. What drives you to do what you do?'

'Sir, I…' Ankit's voice wavered as his throat tightened.

'Go on,' the doctor prompted gently, though the encouragement did little to calm Ankit's nerves.

The room fell into a brief but palpable silence. *Is this*

for real? Ankit thought, feeling blindsided. *Since when do residency interviews include soul-searching questions? Weren't they supposed to test my technical knowledge? How the hell am I supposed to answer this out-of-syllabus question?*

Sensing his hesitation, another panellist spoke up, offering clarification. 'I think what my colleague is asking is—who is Dr Ankit apart from a medical professional?'

Ankit swallowed hard. 'Sir, I am sorry, but I may need some time for this,' he admitted honestly.

The doctors exchanged brief glances before one of them nodded. 'All right, we'll move on to the technical round for now—take your time and come back to it when you're ready.'

For the next 25 minutes, the questions were purely clinical—demanding but expected. Ankit answered with as much precision and composure as he could muster.

Towards the end of the technical round, Dr Gray, who had been quietly observing until now, sat forward and tapped his pen once on the notepad in front of him. 'You're on your inpatient rotation,' he began. 'An undocumented patient. No insurance. Medically stable. There's pressure to discharge—not because it's best for the patient, but because the hospital does not want to carry the cost. What do you do?'

Ankit took a breath before responding.

'I would ask the team to pause. We owe the patient a careful discharge process. That means involving social work, exploring community options and checking if any legal support services are available. If none of that changes the outcome, I would make sure it is all documented. I would not let the discharge be framed as routine when it clearly is not.'

Dr Gray looked up from his notes. 'That is not going to make you popular.'

Ankit gave a slight nod. 'I am not trying to be popular. I am trying to be honest—with myself and with the patient. If we are going to discharge someone into uncertainty, we should at least be transparent about it.'

Dr Gray studied him for a moment. 'You think that is your job?'

'I think it is part of the job. Being a physician is not just about writing orders or managing symptoms. It is also about making sure people are not quietly erased by the system.'

There was a long pause.

'And who taught you that?' Dr Gray asked.

Ankit looked him in the eye. 'Watching what happens when no one does.'

Dr Gray closed the notepad in front of him. 'All right,' he said. 'Thank you. Let's move on.'

Then Dr Hawker spoke up for the first time. 'Do you believe in God, Dr Ankit?' he suddenly asked.

Ankit's fingers tapped nervously against the armrest of his chair as he replied, 'I do believe in humanistic wisdom, sir, but I do not associate myself with any religion or its teachings.'

'But I see a sacred red thread on your wrist,' Dr Hawker pointed out. 'Is that not something a person of faith wears?'

'Well, this, sir, is my mother's placebo,' Ankit replied, a soft smile tugging at the corner of his lips. 'She believes it provides me with safety, which in turn gives her peace of mind. Wearing a thread is a small price to pay for that, sir.'

'Hmmm... Interesting.' After a brief pause, Dr Hawker posed another question. 'Do you know why we conduct interviews even after candidates clear one of the toughest theoretical examinations in the US, along with an equally challenging clinical skills assessment?'

'Because a doctor is much more than a candidate appearing for examinations, sir,' Ankit replied steadily. 'A mere standardized test is not sufficient to evaluate a candidate's eligibility for the programme. For a better, in-depth assessment of a candidate's qualities, interviews like these are essential, sir.'

As he spoke, Ankit couldn't help but wish policymakers in India would realize this as well. The deteriorating educational system shaped by incompetent policymakers had left the healthcare sector in shambles.

'Well answered,' Dr Hawker gave a small nod of approval. 'Last question. Why surgical oncology? And why this institute?'

Ankit felt a sudden tightness in his chest. His throat constricted ever so slightly. He had rehearsed this answer a hundred times before, yet now, speaking the words aloud, he found it difficult to suppress the emotion.

'Sir, I lost my sister to cancer a couple of years ago,' he began softly. 'Her tumour grew rapidly, and before any of us could do anything...we lost her. I can still feel the crushing helplessness I felt back then. It may sound cliché, sir, but I think if I can save someone's life, it might lessen that feeling.

'The pain and suffering my sister endured made me not only understand but also experience how others feel... Her loss shook my sense of omnipotence. It made me realize that medicine isn't about being infallible—it's about learning and searching for answers with humility...

'It is for a deeply personal reason that I applied for the surgical oncology programme at your institution. Dr Silva is a pioneer in the field, and I want to learn from the best.'

4

Running on the Edge

Wing C Cafeteria
Northbridge General Hospital

'Wait for me in the Wing C cafeteria. Will be there in 10 mins. Let's have lunch together. —J'

Ankit read the text from Dr Jindal and slipped his phone back into his pocket. After placing his order, he made his way to an empty table in the cafeteria, wondering how his interview had gone. Had he overdone the personal aspect in his response? How would the panel respond to that? It was difficult to share vulnerabilities, but perhaps that's exactly what they were looking for.

Now that the interview was over, his mind was free to wander. He scanned his surroundings absent-mindedly. The cafeteria, like most of Wing C, was part of a recent addition to the institute's original architecture. The older wings carried a gloomier vibe in comparison.

The tantalizing aroma of food filled the air, tempting him to try something new and delicious. The constant buzz of laughter and chatter hummed in his ears as people moved about. There was something unusual about the people here—they exchanged smiles even if they didn't know each other… Or maybe it was something else—he couldn't quite exactly pinpoint yet.

A loud screech jolted him back to his senses. Dr Jindal had arrived and was pulling out a metal chair at the table.

'So, how did it go?' he asked without preamble.

'I don't know, Dr Jindal. Not sure. The technical round went well; I think I overdid a few questions about ethics.'

'I personally think the technical round is the most important. If that went well, it means you've done good, son. After all, it is the computer that will be assessing you, not the panellists. Ethics is too complex a concept for a machine—it's radially dualistic and hyper-reductionist.' He continued, 'Although, most of the interviews here—regardless of field—are behaviourally designed.'

'It isn't up to the panellists to select?' Ankit asked, confused.

'Not any more,' Dr Jindal shook his head. 'They will rank you based on overall feedback, but it's the algorithm that makes the match. In 1962, Dr Shapley and his colleague Dr Gale introduced the Gale–Shapley algorithm, also known as the deferred acceptance algorithm, to find optimal matches for stable marriages. Over time it found its way into the residency match process and even into systems like the one used by the US Naval Research Laboratory. Shapley later shared the Nobel Prize in 2012 with economist Alvin Roth for its wide-ranging applications,' Dr Jindal regaled the information effortlessly, as if he had just read it that morning.

'I had no idea software was involved in the match process. Thanks for the information, Doctor. You're a big fan of trivia, aren't you? Not many people know such unique and interesting things,' Ankit said, with newfound appreciation for Dr Jindal.

'Well, when you're an Indian living abroad, you're expected to be smart—the smartest person in the room. The West has this positive stereotype about elite Indians—they think we exude culture and wisdom that dates back thousands of years. We know it's not entirely true. I mean, we lost track of that wisdom somewhere along the way as it was passed down for centuries, didn't we? But don't let it bother you now. I read a lot of technological journals; that's why I know these software-related facts and jargon,' Dr Jindal concluded in a matter-of-fact tone.

He pulled out a Tupperware container from his bag and started fiddling with the lid.

What is it with Indians and their Tupperware? Ankit mused, suppressing a smile.

'Sir, on the flight you mentioned something about helping me find accommodation?'

Dr Jindal took forever to open his Tupperware before finally addressing the question.

'Oh yes, about that—we'll sort it out soon; first, I need to invite you before I forget. My wife and I host a Diwali party every year, and we are having one tomorrow. You must come; I'll send you the address and the location—better yet, I'll have you picked up. It's just a five-minute ride uptown from your current accommodation. There will be plenty of Indians there—a great opportunity for you to make connections. Besides, I don't want you spending Diwali alone. You do not have any plans, do you, young man?' Dr Jindal asked.

'No, sir, I don't. Thanks, I'll be there.'

'Also, it is imperative that you make new friends here, especially Indians. Though society here is generally open and accepting, you still need to be careful. Your own people will give you nuanced insight and information. I'll be glad if you're selected.'

Ankit nodded, appreciating the advice.

And then it struck him—what had felt out of place earlier. 'Dr Jindal, I noticed today that most of the leadership here—teachers, managers—are ethnically homogeneous. There aren't many Asians or brown people, or even African Americans, for that matter. Yet, the waiting room was full of South Asian doctors. Is the selection process biased towards us?' Ankit asked.

'Are you surprised? I know they say America is a melting pot of ethnicities, but in reality, it's a bit more complicated in my opinion—especially in our profession. You'll see,' Dr Jindal replied.

'Should I be worried about it?' Ankit asked, worried.

'Well, if the rumours are true, things are changing this time around. And anyway, if your technical round went well—and you're saying it did—I don't think there's much to worry about. Every system has inherent biases; back home, one exam determines your destiny. Here, at least there are many other attributes that count. And it's a better time to be in the US; since the public movement following George Floyd's death, there's been a strong push for diversity, inclusivity, and equity. The fact remains that worrying won't do you any good; I'd say it's futile,' Dr Jindal said.

'It's easy to say not to worry, as if it's in my control, but worries have a special relationship with me; it's an experience that never seems to leave me,' Ankit replied wryly.

Finishing his lunch with a loud burp, Dr Jindal gave Ankit a firm pat on the back before bidding him farewell.

∞

5

Aesthetics

Wing B
Northbridge General Hospital

Dr Pooja Awasthi looked at herself in the washroom mirror and scowled. Apparently, her Pilates class was doing nothing for her. Maybe it was her evening binge drinking habit, or maybe it was just middle age, but the reflection staring back at her was not what she wanted to see. Her fading charm added to her growing second thoughts about the idea of beauty, and she couldn't help but feel distressed.

Adjusting her hair bun, she glanced at her watch. 2.35 p.m. Lunchtime.

As she headed towards the cafeteria, the shrillest scream she had ever heard froze her in her tracks. It was like a banshee going into labour. Was it coming from the maternity ward? No, that was on the other side of the wing—this scream was coming from the emergency ward. Dumping her lunch plans, Pooja sprinted towards the sound and located its source soon enough.

The emergency ward was alive with a cacophony of sounds—the low hum of fluorescent lights, the sharp echo of footsteps on sterile tiles and the relentless beeping of monitors. A woman in her mid-20s was being wheeled in on a stretcher, her distressed screams filling the air. She clutched her stomach, crying out in unbearable pain, her face twisted in agony; her skin was pale and clammy with sweat.

'What is it?' Pooja asked the nurse pushing the stretcher.

'Just came in. Extreme abdominal pain,' the nurse replied.

'Why wasn't she given painkillers in the ambulance?'

'She was, but no painkiller or analgesic is working,' the nurse informed Pooja.

'What did you give?'

'One shot of a painkiller. When that didn't work, we gave her Tramadol. It didn't help either.'

'All right, let me see.'

'Dr Pooja, what's your diagnosis?' her colleague, Dr Andy, asked as he joined them.

'Her stomach seems swollen with gas. I suspect an intestinal obstruction. We need a CT scan immediately,' Pooja said.

'They are cleaning the scan lab right now. A patient vomited in there. Can we wait?'

The woman's screams grew louder, her body trembling from the pain.

'No, I don't think we can. Let's get an abdominal X-ray in the meantime,' Pooja said.

This is bizarre. None of the painkillers are working. What kind of obstruction can this possibly be? she thought as they

Aesthetics

waited for the X-ray results.

When the results arrived, they only baffled her further. Usually, gases turn dark on an X-ray, but in this case, the areas were plain black. *This isn't gas; this is something else,* she thought.

Medicine is often taught from books, but real knowledge comes from experience—countless hours spent on hospital floors, exposure to raw human suffering and insights gleaned from unusual cases. It was moments like these that Pooja drew upon her subconscious library of experience.

And then it struck her.

A memory surfaced of a class she had attended a long time ago. She could still see Professor Sharma holding up a dried-up lump of hair retrieved from a patient's food pipe, waving it dramatically for the class to see.

'Andy, check her scalp,' Pooja directed. 'Anything unusual there?'

'Wait, let me—what? Scalp? What on earth has that got to do with her intestines?' Dr Andy raised an eyebrow.

'Just check, please; I'll explain later,' she insisted.

Andy shrugged and leaned over the patient. Moments later, he looked up, eyes wide. 'Doctor, she's got big bald patches! What does that mean? Is she under some kind of treatment?' Dr Andy asked, baffled.

'Trichobezoar,' Pooja murmured.

Dr Andy looked at her with scepticism. 'Wait—you're saying she's got a bezoar? From hair?' he asked incredulously. 'That seems kind of unbelievable. Let me check what the radiologist has to say.'

He turned to his computer and began typing furiously. 'Let's see…' His expression shifted to wonder as he read the report. 'It says here that the indentation in the stomach lining, while clinical correlation is needed, reflects hair-like particles obstructing the pyloric region—the area where the stomach connects to the intestine. Most likely a foreign body… Hair follicles!' He spun around, staring at Pooja with open admiration, a wide smile spreading across his face.

'Unbelievable! You were able to develop so many differentials and rule them out. Genius diagnosis, Dr Pooja,' Dr Andy said.

'Get her to the Endoscopy Lab immediately; I'll prepare for the procedure to remove it,' Pooja said.

A few hours later, Pooja went to see the patient, who seemed extremely exhausted but visibly relieved. Noticing the faint smile on her face, Pooja briefly explained what had happened. 'Trichotillomania is an impulse control disorder where individuals compulsively pluck out their own hair and, in some cases, eat it. The ingested hair often collects in the stomach, forming a large, indigestible mass called a trichobezoar, which sometimes obstructs the intestine.'

'You're lucky,' Pooja said softly. 'We were able to remove the hair mass without surgery. No scars.'

The woman's eyes welled slightly with emotion as she acknowledged ongoing issues with worry and anxiety. Then she added, 'Thank you, Doctor. I thought I was going to die. The pain was unbearable, and I didn't think I'd be able to handle it.'

'You did great,' Pooja reassured the young woman. 'Don't worry about anything else right now. Your mother is outside; I will call her in.'

The patient's face wavered between gratitude and vulnerability. 'My mother doesn't know,' she admitted. 'And I don't know how to tell her. I hope you can help me with that. I don't want her to be upset… But maybe it's time I get help from a professional. I think I need it.'

Pooja nodded. 'We'll get you the help you need. You have already taken the first step by admitting to it.'

Stepping out of the room, Pooja requested Dr Andy to call someone from the Psychiatry Department.

'Her mother wants to thank you; she is waiting outside,' Dr Andy informed Pooja softly.

Pooja shook her head lightly, already walking away. 'Umm, Dr Andy, can you take care of that, please? I am going to have my lunch.'

As she walked towards the cafeteria, she pulled out her phone. A text message from Dr Jindal from the Anaesthesia Department blinked on her screen.

'Diwali party tomorrow at my place. Be there at 19:00, please. —J'

6

Reunion

Dr Jindal's House

Ankit adjusted his blazer and, with a final glance at his hairstyle on his phone, walked towards Dr Jindal's house. A chauffeured limo had picked him up from the hotel and dropped him in the driveway. Dr Jindal lived in one of the poshest neighbourhoods in the city. Like a children's video game machine in an arcade, his house was lit up by thousands of mini-LED lights snaking across the façade, giving it a festive look. The rest of the block was enveloped in darkness and radio silence, making the house seem even more striking in its ephemeral festivity.

'There you are, boy,' Dr Jindal greeted him at the door, accompanied by a beautiful lady of short stature. 'This is Mrs Jindal. I told her about you yesterday, and she was looking forward to meeting you.'

Dressed in a gaudy silk saree, Mrs Jindal was adorned with gold and diamond jewellery from head to toe. It was probably her benign attempt to conform to a curated concept of festivity, yet she remained oblivious to how the dazzling display of her ornaments could stir both envy and fascination among her guests. That's the thing about ambivalence—the metaphysical philosophy behind the idea of festivals, once deeply embedded in cultural heritage, was now diluted and overshadowed by material possessions and extravagant seven-course meals. Another conundrum of migration is the expectation of an egalitarian world on the other side, one that will assimilate your identity. Yet it's a terrifying thought for many who are unwilling to learn or adopt the prevailing cultures that create the very opportunities that enabled them to move.

After exchanging greetings and pleasantries, Ankit walked in, entering the courtyard. The space was buzzing with guests and waiters, with the ladies flaunting their lavish outfits, over-accessorized with jewellery just like Mrs Jindal.

The courtyard was easily at least twice the size of his entire house back home. *If the courtyard alone is so grand, how massive would the whole house be?* Ankit wondered.

One end had been transformed into a barbecue station, with a large grill installed along the counter; in the adjoining corner, an outdoor bar stood adorned with an ornate wooden wine cabinet. Opposite the entrance, a glass partition separated the courtyard from the lounge area of the house, marking the boundary where indoor ended and outdoor began. Inside, along the far wall, an extravagant buffet was laid out, with some guests already helping themselves to dinner. Across from the buffet stood a huge temple with idols of various gods and goddesses, some looming larger than others.

It seems Indians prioritize the gods of wealth and good luck everywhere, even in America, Ankit mused. *How ironic. For thousands of years, our forefathers and foremothers focused on internal, mindful awakening rather than external dreaming. Now, the ideas of productivity, access, power and surplus have overshadowed conventional wisdom, and the imbalance is visible in the form of sweet deception.*

The entire courtyard and lounge were illuminated by low yellow bulbs, casting a glittering golden glow that further enhanced the opulence of the gold jewellery worn by the women. The ceremonious rituals had already ended by the time Ankit arrived, but out of courtesy, he decided to linger by the bar for some time before moving towards the buffet. Holding a glass of Shirley Temple in one hand and a piece of paneer tikka in the other, he surveyed the setting. His gaze landed on Dr Jindal, who was talking animatedly to a group of three, two of whom appeared Indian. Catching Ankit's eye, Dr Jindal beckoned him over.

Ankit walked across the courtyard and stepped into the lavish living room, his eyes sweeping over the high ceilings, the crystal chandelier and the floor-to-ceiling windows that overlooked the twinkling city skyline. The faint hum of conversation and gentle clinking of glasses filled the air.

Dr Jindal introduced the group of men standing near the fireplace. 'Ankit, meet Dr Shashi, Dr Goldstein and Dr Ahmed,' he said. 'Dr Shashi is from your town—Palamgarh. Dr Goldstein is from Israel and Dr Ahmed is from Pakistan, but I have forgotten the exact place.'

The men exchanged nods—polite but distant. Ankit

noticed Dr Goldstein swirling a glass of red wine in his hand, while Dr Ahmed adjusted his cufflinks, his expression unreadable.

Dr Jindal exhaled slowly, his gaze drifting across the room. 'I was telling these gentlemen,' he gestured at the opulence around them—the extravagant décor, the sleek black limo still visible outside the glass doors, 'that this is the product of a capitalistic, individualistic society. This house, that car, this lifestyle—it all comes at a cost.'

He leaned against the grand piano, running a hand over its polished surface as he continued. 'Everything boils down to your ability to make an informed choice, placing your goals above everything else. It's more about I, me and myself—without even knowing who I am or what I want. Staying relevant in this society demands maintaining this lifestyle. The parameters keep shifting and people buy loads of things they don't need, all to sustain the grand illusion.'

Ankit glanced around at the guests scattered throughout the room—laughing, clinking glasses, engaged in hushed conversations. The drinks flowed freely, the glasses never seeming to empty. The weight of Dr Jindal's words settled heavily in his mind.

'Ultimately, every commodity disappoints,' Dr Jindal carried on, his voice quieter now. 'That's why, after an hour of drinking, these people will start reminiscing about times when they had nothing—when the simplest pleasures meant everything. You see, pleasure isn't in acquiring something. It's in yearning for it. The moment you get what you want, the magic fades.'

A long silence followed, broken only by the crackling fireplace.

Dr Jindal sighed, rubbing his temples. 'One day, when you're old, you'll realize that this lifestyle made you miss out on so much. But by then, it'll be too late. Value is an intrinsic concept. There is nothing at the top, son.' He fixed Ankit with a sharp gaze. 'I repeat, there is nothing at the top. It's much scarier up there. And very lonely.'

Ankit shifted his weight, unsure how to respond. 'That's a deep thought, Dr Jindal,' he said finally. 'Can you elaborate on the last line?'

Dr Jindal's lips curled into a small, knowing smile. 'I think I can explain it better with an example.' He straightened and took a measured sip of his whisky before continuing.

'On Easter Island, there's a rock that tourists come to see. It's ugly, really. Just a weathered stone with a hole in it. But when the wind passes through, it makes a whooshing noise, which is why they call it the "Stone Trumpet". Ancient Easter Islanders believed this rock had divine power. They thought it granted fertility in women and ensured prosperous crops. For generations, tribes fought over it, killing and dying just to possess it. The victorious tribe would hold the rock—until another tribe attacked and took it. Likely, thousands of people have died for that rock.'

Dr Jindal set his glass down on the piano lid with a quiet clink. 'Today, that same rock is worthless. Just a mildly interesting tourist attraction.' He spread his hands. 'Things are only as valuable as we make them.'

Ankit let out a slow breath, absorbing the story. He glanced at the limo outside once more, then smirked. 'Not sure if I understood all of it,' he admitted, chuckling, 'but I know one thing: if I had a limo, I'd never take a Greyhound bus to work.'

Laughter rippled through the group, breaking the sombre mood. Dr Jindal shook his head, a small, amused smile flitting across his face. 'Perhaps, Ankit, but give it time. One day, even the limo might feel like just another rock on Easter Island.'

He leaned back slightly, resting his elbow on the piano. His eyes grew distant as he continued, his voice softer, more reflective. 'My friends were more free-spirited back then. And much more talkative. We used to advise our co-passengers. It's a pity you can't do that any more, thanks to bureaucracy, but then, we spoke with all kinds of people. In a sense, Greyhounds are to America what public roadways are in India. They're cheap, they're fast and they're full of people from everywhere. Greyhounds are the wagon of people of all colours.'

'That's a very interesting observation, Dr Jindal, but you still haven't answered my original question,' Dr Shashi chimed in. 'Why do you think Americans open their doors for us Indians, Pakistanis and Israelis to come train here and practise?'

'Ah yes, I was coming to that, Dr Shashi; don't think I was ignoring your question. But before I answer that'—Dr Jindal's eyes sharpened as he turned towards Ankit—'Ankit, why did you decide to come train here in the USA? Give me a short and crisp one-line answer.'

'Well, no offence, but the whole system back home is in shambles. And by system, I mean the healthcare system as well as the education system,' Ankit replied.

'Exactly!' Dr Jindal pointed at him emphatically. 'You see, manufacturing a doctor—as I like to call it—is an expensive process that also requires a lot of human resources. The government must spend vast sums of money on medical education. We, on the other hand, are substitutes for that. For postgraduate training, the federal government spends millions, of which you and I are the beneficiaries. So, it's a mixed bag and no one wants to reform it, since the status quo suits many.'

Ankit nodded in understanding.

'The cherry on the cake,' Dr Jindal continued, 'is our rotten system. We don't need many incentives. Fresh postgraduates in India, without clinical experience, start with salaries that are laughably low. For those who have established entities or have family members in the healthcare business, it's a soft landing, even though they are just as inexperienced as the others. Don't get me wrong—the merit does work, but it's delayed for decades. And the public psyche? Well, they are happy to pay for goods but reluctant to pay for services. It's a cultural factor. Not everyone can afford delayed gratification; after all, they also have families to care for.'

He exhaled sharply, swirling the amber liquid in his glass. 'It's an irony, really. The fact that not many German or French doctors immigrate to the US tells you something is not right. Young, budding physicians with no family background, funds or backing find it difficult to navigate the system to live a life of dignity—for themselves and their families—given the long time it takes to complete training. The real shock comes when you complete postgraduate training, only to discover that life is now more complicated, with dependent family members and mounting expectations.'

Dr Jindal's voice grew heavier. 'The options for research are limited, harassment from seniors and management is ubiquitous and then you have media reports of mob violence against professionals when outcomes are undesirable. Doctors from some countries are only too happy to leave everything behind and chase the great American dream. The West has built an immigration system where both parties, in tangible terms, are mutual beneficiaries.'

With that, Dr Jindal drained the last of his whisky and, with a polite nod, excused himself to greet other guests.

Dr Shashi watched him go, then turned to Ankit with a curious expression. 'Interesting character, that Dr Jindal. Where did you meet him, Ankit?'

'On a flight yesterday, sir. I was en route for my interview.'

Dr Shashi smiled faintly. 'Also, drop the "sir", please. It's a funny thing we Indians do—call others Sir and Ma'am. I used to do it too,' he added with a chuckle.

'I am so traumatized by this, Dr Shashi. One of our newer faculty members in my college back home, Dr Banerjee, had asked postgraduate physicians to call him by his first name, and what happened after that is a story. He got disciplined; obviously, they could not do it directly, but there are many tools that core faculty could use to harass him. He was so vulnerable that he left without saying a word because they threatened to give him negative references. And as far as I remember, he was not paid for three months. Last I knew, Dr Banerjee was in Singapore. He was outstanding—spoke his mind and was loved by everyone, except a few higher-ups,' Ankit said, shaking his head.

'No wonder Socrates was sentenced to death,' Dr Shashi said, chuckling.

Ankit let out a dry chuckle before shifting his attention to Dr Ahmed, who had been quietly listening to the conversation.

'How long have you been living here, Doctor?' Ankit asked.

'Long enough to agree with Dr Jindal,' Dr Ahmed replied with a wry smile. 'In India, people are vulnerable to products that are elevated to pedestals and are easier to regulate due to the fear of steep falls. Similarly, people here sometimes blame us for stealing their jobs—but it's more directed at tech workers than doctors. There are banned organizations like the Proud Boys, the KKK and plenty of conservative groups that hate people of other ethnicities. They probably feel threatened. Ultimately, it all boils down to our human tendency to live in tribes. You will rarely find us living somewhere in the countryside. We always stick to close-knit communities in major cities.' He paused, his eyes narrowing slightly. 'This bunch of tribal thinking sounds dangerously close to the Lebensraum notion of Hitler. Sorry to bring it up, Doctor, but you're familiar with it, right?'

'I am,' Ankit nodded. 'It's just a fine example of mass brainwashing. You see it everywhere, even in democratic countries.'

'To that, I can agree. In Pakistan, we are brainwashed about Indians. When I first came here, I used to stay away from them.' He glanced at Dr Shashi with a warm smile. 'What an irony! One of my best friends now is an Indian. Isn't that right, Dr Shashi?'

Dr Shashi replied with a smile of his own. 'And most of this indoctrination happens in early childhood—before the faculty of reasoning is even developed.'

'It does, indeed,' Dr Ahmed agreed. Then his eyes narrowed. 'Are you all right, Ankit? You're as white as parchment—as if you've seen a ghost!'

It *was* a ghost he had seen. Or so Ankit thought.

It had been fleeting—a glance, no more—as he idly scanned the room. But then he'd seen those eyes. His stomach clenched.

Could it be her? he thought.

'I'm not feeling well. I need to use the washroom, I think. Excuse me, gentlemen,' Ankit muttered, barely managing to keep his voice steady.

Without waiting for a response, he turned and walked away, his heart pounding in his chest.

7

Tour de Force

Staff Lounge
Northbridge General Hospital

Rachel was enjoying her brief tea break in the staff lounge when Amy from the Plastic and Reconstructive Surgery department popped in. As they chatted, it wasn't long before the conversation turned to the enigmatic and fascinating Dr Silva.

'I saw your doctor on television last night,' Amy declared, her excitement evident. 'She was phenomenal! The break room was buzzing about it. It's incredible how she's put our hospital on the map. Ten years ago, no one even knew we existed, and now we're on national television thanks to her work.'

Rachel smiled, her pride unmistakable. She found Dr Silva's journey, as unorthodox as it was, truly inspiring. It was hard to believe that someone who started off so modestly had risen to such prominence. By all accounts, Dr Silva had been an ordinary student—reserved, shy and easily overlooked in a sea of louder personalities. A family friend who'd attended school with her once told Rachel that young Silva rarely spoke unless spoken to.

Her focus was on her studies and she seemed content to blend into the background, which only made her ethnicity—being one of the few people of colour in a mostly homogeneous school—stand out even more. Her professional journey wasn't much smoother either. When she announced her intention to specialize in surgical oncology, a field dominated by men, she faced a lot of scepticism. 'Why not paediatrics or gynaecology? Those are better suited for women,' she was told repeatedly.

Rather than react with anger or indignation, Dr Silva always held her ground with calm confidence. Her strength didn't come from making a scene; instead, it was her quiet determination and relentless pursuit of excellence that left a mark on everyone she met. She wasn't the type to network aggressively or chase after opportunities; instead, it seemed that opportunities found her because of her unparalleled expertise. It was as if the universe couldn't ignore her brilliance.

Dr Silva had become a pioneer in healthcare, particularly in surgical oncology, and was widely regarded as one of the foremost leaders in the field. But her influence extended beyond medicine. She had also become a formidable force in healthcare policy reforms, spearheading initiatives that addressed both systemic inequalities and underserved populations. She chaired a prominent commission advocating for the rights of the hyper-marginalized, fighting to ensure that every individual received care regardless of their background or status.

Her commitment to justice wasn't just professional—it

was personal. She had challenged discriminatory remarks during board meetings, citing evidence and first-hand experience. At a community event, when young immigrant women were dismissed by doctors as 'unimportant cases', she'd sat down with them, listened and ensured they got the care they needed. Many believed her fierce advocacy stemmed from personal history—but no one had ever dared to ask.

'Don't you feel intimidated by her? She's a real stickler for rules, and everyone in the hospital knows how hard it is to work with her,' Amy asked, curious.

'She's meticulous to a fault,' Rachel admitted. 'Some call her compulsive, but it's more about her commitment to precision. She expects the same rigour from everyone, and while that can be exhausting, it's also what makes her work exceptional.'

Rachel recalled a recent committee meeting where Dr Silva had led a heated discussion on how to allocate the J2 research grants, which are similar to the prestigious K-12 grants. With the university dean, the educational chair and other high-ranking officials in attendance, the atmosphere was charged with differing opinions. Dr Silva's incisive questions cut through the noise, zeroing in on how the funds were actually being utilized. She was relentless in her pursuit of transparency and accountability, making a strong case for open-access publications. 'Research funded by public money should benefit the public,' she often asserted.

Amy nodded, visibly impressed. 'It's rare to see someone stick to their principles in such a competitive field. Doesn't that make her unpopular?'

Rachel chuckled, her lips curling into a smile. 'Oh, absolutely! But that's also why she commands so much respect. Everyone knows she can't be swayed by money or power. She once turned down a prestigious position at a renowned think tank because she felt their practices were unethical. She told me, "You don't need power to do good. You just need to be willing." That's the kind of person she is.'

Amy raised an eyebrow, clearly intrigued. 'She sounds like a force to be reckoned with. Does she have any other quirks?'

Rachel's smile deepened, as though she was about to divulge a secret. 'She's unpredictable in some ways. She might decline something everyone assumes she'll agree to, and it's not always clear why. One minute she's debating the philosophical implications of a paper, the next she's dismissing it because the font isn't the right aesthetic. You never quite know which way she'll lean. But when it comes to her research, she's unwavering. She won't publish anything until she's absolutely certain it's perfect. Her team hates it—especially when she sends them back to the drawing board because she's decided the margins need to be 0.5 mm wider—but the results speak for themselves.'

Rachel paused, looking thoughtful. 'There's something about the way she asks questions, too. She never just accepts the obvious answer. I remember once she spent hours arguing with a colleague about the implications of a single word in a paper. They thought she was being pedantic, but she was right. That one word changed the whole meaning. It's why people trust her so much. She doesn't settle for "good enough". It's either all in or nothing at all.'

Rachel then shared a story about a physician from a prestigious institute who had questioned Dr Silva's approach during a heated phone call. She had calmly but firmly countered every argument, pointing out that the so-called 'standard' practices were often more about tradition than evidence. 'Just because it's coming from a big name doesn't make it right,' she had said, a statement that left her challenger momentarily speechless.

As their break ended, Amy shook her head in admiration. 'She sounds like someone who's not just good at what she does but also someone who makes everyone around her better. That's rare.'

Rachel smiled. 'She is. And that's why, despite her quirks, we're all better for working with her. She's not just a physician, she's a *tour de force*.'

༺༻

8

Unfinished Juxtaposition

Dr Jindal's House

Was it really her? No, I must have imagined it.

Ankit was sweating. He washed his face and looked around. Even the washroom had that glittery golden light. *Is it a rich-people thing?* he wondered. *Do they all like dim lights or is it just a way to save on electricity bills?* He stared at the commode, perplexed. *Even the water seal is too high. Is it supposed to be like this, or did I flush wrong?*

Flustered, Ankit walked out of the washroom—and stumbled right into her.

It really is her; bloody hell! 'Pooja?'

'Ankit? Hi!'

'Hi, I was…uh…not expecting you here. I mean, what a lovely surprise!' Ankit fumbled with his words, his smile growing wider by the second.

'Yeah, it is! It's been so long. You have changed quite a bit, I see,' Pooja remarked, scanning him.

'Oh, you mean I've become fat? Yeah, I know. I need to cut down on carbs, I guess. It's impressive you even recognized me.'

'I was watching you when you entered; it's hard not to recognize that smile.'

Ankit took a long pause. Too long. Long enough for it to feel awkward—his lips frozen in a half-smile, his jaw slightly slack. It was funny how humans are anthropologically prepared to tackle attacks but crumble under the weight of attention and praise.

For so many years he had tried to find Pooja, but she was a modern ghost.

'Are you not on social media, Pooja?'

'I'm not,' she replied, her voice carrying a mix of pride and hesitation. 'At least, not openly.'

Ankit raised an eyebrow. 'Not openly? What does that mean?'

She smirked. 'I had a profile. But in disguise. Hidden, covert, completely incognito. No one can find me. Or at least, that's what I tell myself.'

That's why I could not find her, Ankit thought. 'So, you're stalking people from the shadows?'

'Not stalking. Observing,' she corrected, giving him a pointed look. 'And honestly, I know when someone's looking for me too. It's subtle—things like the institutions they're tied to or the connections they make. I can piece it together. It's like a grown-up game of peekaboo.'

'Peekaboo?' Ankit laughed.

'Yes,' Pooja replied. 'You can't get away from it, can't stay away, can't ignore it. It's addictive in this weird, quiet way. And let's be real—it's all just FOMO. Fear of missing out, even when you don't want to be found.'

Ankit shook his head, grinning. 'You're creeping me out, Pooja.'

She smiled. 'We all do it, Ankit. Some of us are just better at hiding it. But you clearly are not. So, should I infer you tried looking for me, you stalker?' she teased.

Noticing Ankit's ears turning red, she added, 'Oh, stop getting awkward, Ankit. I'm just messing with you! I'm not on social media any more. I was, but then I realized it's just a platform people use to showcase their edited lives. It creates this fancy, filtered version of everything, blurring the lines of reality.'

'Well said. The lines demarcating humans and technology are getting blurred every day—the post-human era,' Ankit mused. 'But you sound much more confident than the Pooja I knew years ago. And a tad bit cynical.'

'Ah, sugar-coated cynicism and sarcasm. I like that.'

'Seriously, you are much more confident. And there's a different glow to you. How's everything?'

'I'd attribute that glow to peripheral vasodilation and disinhibition caused by excessively expensive champagne,' Pooja replied with a smirk. 'I also make daily trips to the gym and do a little bit of swimming,' she added, half-stammering. Then, with a casual shrug, she continued, 'And if by "everything" you mean my marriage, well, that didn't work out. My other half had some problems adjusting to a free-thinking and confident woman like me; he wanted a meek and simple wife who'd follow him blindly.'

'Relatable.'

'How is it relatable to you? Are you a liberal woman as well?' Pooja laughed.

Damn, that laughter, Ankit thought. *It's still as captivating as ever.*

'Very funny. No, I mean, I relate to the guy here. Truth be told, I think I also had a problem with confident and independent women. They intimidated me. I wanted someone submissive and conformist like my mother. But I realized much later that the way she was—it was not because she wanted to be that way, but because she had to be. Maybe that's how you survive in a patriarchal society,' Ankit explained softly.

'Hmm. So, did you marry that girl next-door who was super into you?' Pooja asked.

'You remember her? No, I didn't. I did start talking to her but did not accept the marriage proposal from her family.'

'Why?'

'Well, we hardly had anything in common. She was into travelling and binge-watching celebrity news and gossip, and I realized that although I was infatuated with her beauty, I'd never be in love with her. It would never have worked out between us.'

'So, were you in love when you proposed to someone else?'

'You're still the same blunt woman I knew years ago. Cutting through the bullshit and arriving at the point like a boss.'

'Well, some things never change, do they?' Pooja said,

her eyes glimmering with mischief.

'No, they don't, I guess.' Ankit shifted slightly. 'Umm, should we be talking about this, Pooja? It's been so many years.'

'Chill, I'm just pulling your leg,' she laughed, masking the sudden pang of regret in her chest. She had thought about reaching out to him so many times, but she never did. And now, she knew it would be a lifelong regret.

It's strange how we yearn more for what we don't get; human life is so centred around loss. Once we get what we want, it becomes unwanted and loses its importance.

Sensing the conversation teetering on the edge of awkwardness, Ankit decided not to respond. Instead, he smiled softly and gestured towards an empty table in the decked-up lawn. 'Shall we?'

Pooja nodded and followed him. 'What did you do after medical school? Where were you?' Pooja wanted to have all the conversations they had missed out on over the years, all at once. She had missed talking to him.

'After I returned home for my internship, Dia—my sister—fell sick. It started with vague symptoms. But I knew it was serious. We consulted doctors at one of the premier institutes, but the conditions there were terrible. Patients were crammed into small compartments like cattle. No one cared whether a patient lived or died. They asked for ₹10 lakh upfront for the resection of Dia's hepatoblastoma. We could not manage to put together that kind of money. If you aren't rich or don't know someone in power, you are as good as gone. There was no law, no legislation, no one to help us. We lost Dia to her illness,' Ankit said, his voice cracking slightly as he looked down at his hands.

'Ankit, I'm really sorry for your loss. I never met her but I can hear the pain in your voice. May she rest in peace, wherever she is.' Pooja pictured a lonely, grieving Ankit and felt an ache in her chest. She wanted to reach out and hold him, to tell him it would all be okay.

'I spiralled into a depression after that. When you lose someone you love, the pain is relentless, difficult to cope with. And before you know it, a part of you shuts off and you're drowning in it. It was affecting everyone in my family, especially Pari, my niece. She had already lost her mother, and now I was slipping away too. It took me months, but one day, something shifted. I started reading books—books outside of medicine. Literature, humanities, philosophy... It overwhelmed me, the wisdom in those words.

'That was a turning point for me. I realized grieving was essential, but I had a duty to live—to fulfil my responsibilities and find meaning in this life, somehow. I prepared for a year and got into one of the top postgraduate colleges in India. I tried to dissociate from the pain by keeping myself busy.'

'And how did you end up here?' Pooja asked. But what she really wanted to know was whether he had grieved her absence. Had he missed her too? But it felt selfish to ask. He had gone through so much, and all she could think about was herself.

'After PG, I decided to apply for the resident training programme in the Surgical Oncology Department of

Unfinished Juxtaposition 57

Northbridge General Hospital. Yesterday, on my way to the interview, I met Dr Jindal. He was kind enough to invite me to the party tonight. How do you know him?' Ankit asked. What he really wanted to know was why she was here, now, after all these years. And what if her return crumbled everything he had worked so hard to rebuild? The questions lingered, unspoken.

'Oh, I work at Northbridge too,' Pooja replied. 'Emergency Department in Wing B.'

Ankit blinked. *Of all the hospitals in the world...*

'Wow, oncology,' she continued, 'you'll be working under one of the most famous doctors in the world. Dr Silva is a legend.'

Pooja smiled at Ankit. The party no longer interested her. Only Ankit did. She wanted to keep talking, to catch up on every lost year. 'Let's go for a walk. It's so noisy here,' she suggested, trying hard to keep her heart from bursting with overwhelming emotion. 'And I want to hear more about your PG college,'

They exited the house and started walking down the block, Ankit recounting his experiences.

'Believe me when I say it was a very different experience from medical school. It was brutal. The competition was like nothing I'd ever seen. People studied for 10 hours a day, devouring books by foreign authors. I don't know why the Indian authors were largely dismissed. There was this perception that their work was inferior. And no one wanted to write either. A professor I admired once said, "Every bookshop has a cheaper, photocopied version of the original literature, and that's what students buy."

'Piracy was killing home-grown knowledge. No one wanted to invest in Indian authors when they could just copy Western ones. It made me wonder—when knowledge isn't shared, it dies with the brilliant minds that create it. Most of the time, we were left to teach ourselves because the department was understaffed due to unfilled positions.'

Pooja nodded. 'Yeah, we refer to international authors all the time to keep up with global standards. Most of the evidence is based on Western patients—it doesn't always apply here. What's missing is the nuance of what's normative for us. We need more examples from real-world clinical encounters, drawn from our own population. Without that, we're just approximating Western evidence and applying it blindly.'

'Exactly,' Ankit agreed, his eyes lighting up with passion. 'I once listened to this interesting podcast where a scientist from the West was asked, "Why is there no vaccine for the deadly Ebola virus in Africa?", to which he answered candidly, "It's a shame, but when 50 people from the developed world get it, then the vaccine will come." It hit me then—this brutal, casual indifference to suffering when it's not close to home.'

He shook his head and continued, 'And you know what's worse? Back home, I saw doctors following international protocols that hadn't even been tested on Indian patients yet. I remember this one time—' he paused, his voice hardening, 'a famous Japanese doctor visited us for some event and was allowed to operate on a patient without a licence to practise in India. That is illegal and a punishable crime. The patient passed away, and they hushed it all up. Meanwhile, Indian doctors who go abroad can't even step into the OPD without a valid licence. The double standards are sickening.'

'It's a little different in the West. Here, you might start by volunteering at a hospital, just observing how things are done. Then you apply for formal training. Only once you're a trainee, working under strict supervision, are you even allowed to get involved in actual treatment. Even then, the supervising physician bears the responsibility and only grants more autonomy as you progress through training successfully,' Pooja explained. 'But... What did you do then?' she added, appalled by the incident.

'Nothing. I could do nothing about it,' Ankit replied flatly.

Pooja frowned. 'The Ankit I knew in medical school would never have done nothing about it. You were the rebel—the one who took on the system. What changed?'

'After losing Dia, I definitely wasn't the same Ankit any more. When I got there, I still had some fire in me. I thought I'd fight the system. But seeing it from the inside... It changed me completely. I witnessed things I would not have believed if I hadn't seen them with my own eyes. The political influence... It's insane.'

'Tell me about it,' Pooja urged. She felt lighter somehow, talking to Ankit. As though a sliver of her loneliness was slipping away with each word.

Ankit's gaze darkened. 'There was this one time when Dr Kumar, our department head, received direct orders from the CM's office. The CM was visiting the hospital, supposedly for some treatment. All surgeries were postponed, patients were sidelined—people with life-threatening conditions were made to wait—just so the hospital could roll out the red carpet for him. You know what happened then? The CM didn't even stay for any treatment; he just dragged Dr Kumar along as a mere chaperone to Singapore, where he sought "world-class" treatment.'

Ankit's voice hardened. 'Two people died that day as their surgeries had been cancelled. And something inside me died as well. I was the one who had to face the families and inform them about the last-minute cancellations. I will never forget the look in their eyes—anger, helplessness, disbelief.'

Pooja looked aghast. 'I am surprised nobody said anything. This could never have happened here, not in the Western world I've known. Individual agency still holds weight—there are strong institutional checks and balances. Someone would have complained, and there would have been a serious investigation. Sure, many high-profile people still get special treatment, but not at the cost of others' lives. And if something like this happened, social justice, by and large, would be impartial.'

Ankit let out a bitter chuckle. 'Nobody cared; that was the problem. Our seniors from medical school were also there, struggling like the rest of us. They were too busy surviving to fight the system. I saw them—overworked, underpaid and burnt out. Working extra shifts for peanuts. I don't blame them for not saying anything;

we were all slugging through six-day weeks, clinging to our one day off for binge-booze parties on Sundays, and then hitting repeat.

'That was life; it was all we did. They were content with it, but I knew that life was not for me. I couldn't settle for it. I realized that if I wanted it to be different, I had to let go of the fear of challenging my own beliefs. I had to be willing to think differently, even when it clashed with everything I thought I knew. It was lonely, though. Taking the risk to think... It was emotionally painful and nerve-racking but also cathartic,' he concluded.

For the first time in forever, he didn't feel lonely. Talking to Pooja brought a warmth he hadn't felt in years.

Pooja smiled faintly. 'Yeah, I know you well enough to get you're not meant for an environment like that. Honestly, I don't think anyone is. Here too, after a vehicle accident involving a 30-hour sleep-deprived trainee in 2003, there was massive reform. They introduced Maggie's Law—strict restrictions on trainee hours. It's tragic how many lives are lost before the system finally changes.'

Pooja's mind wandered. She thought how easy it would have been to be a trainee with Ankit by her side. The lives they could have lived.

'I met a very interesting character there—Johnny. Want to hear about him?' Ankit, sensing a shift in Pooja's expression, tried to steer the conversation in a different direction. He was surprised at how easy it was to talk to her, even after all these years.

'Go ahead, I'm all ears.'

'Johnny was a ward boy—a medical technician—but I

swear, he was the most talented colleague I've ever worked with. He could diagnose perforations, appendicitis, even Merkel's, without any clinical investigation. Talent, sixth sense, call it what you want. The only reason he wasn't a doctor was because of the system; he was from a lower caste, and a lack of resources made it impossible for him to pursue medicine. All the students learnt so much from him that we called him "Professor Johnny". He was the one who pushed me to apply for a residency programme abroad. He said I'd be systematically throttled otherwise—psychologically. It's because of him I'm here today.'

'Sounds like a lovely chap, and I'm glad he pushed you. Otherwise, we wouldn't be standing here tonight, talking after all these years.' She paused, then added, 'Why are you smiling?'

'Oh, I just recalled something. A very funny incident, but it's a long story.'

'We have the whole night, Ankit… Unless you have some other plans.'

'Nope, no other plans. All right'—he took a breath, then started narrating—'so this is an old story Johnny told me once. Remember the CM incident? Well, this time, Dr Kumar was whisked away by the coal minister to attend his son's wedding. Turns out, at his daughter's wedding, the guests got so drunk, they rioted. Chairs were flying, people were brawling—it was a complete mess. So this time, he insisted Dr Kumar be with a backup medical unit on standby, just in case.

'So, while he was away, a new trainee was left in

charge of handling all the high-profile patients. It was his rotten luck that on that very day, a relative of the CM walked in. He completely bypassed all protocols, strutted in like he owned the place and announced that he had acute abdominal pain.'

'What happened then?' Pooja asked, engrossed in the story.

Ankit smirked. 'In reality? He was faking it, trying to avoid an arrest for a road rage incident. Cited medical reasons to avoid jail time.'

Pooja burst into laughter. 'Oh my God! What was the diagnosis?'

'Gas after a five-course meal. Johnny decided to give him "VIP" treatment; with the help of that new trainee, he hatched a prank. He told the guy to lie down on the examination table.'

'Then?'

'They made him wait—for 30 whole minutes. Johnny was so excited for this part. That man had probably never waited for anyone in his entire life. They watched him squirm on that table, his anger barely contained. Then, finally, they walked in and, after some examination, diagnosed him with an emergent case of testicular torsion. The trainee in charge told Johnny to prepare him for surgery.'

'Don't tell me he bought that!' Pooja gasped, covering her mouth as laughter threatened to spill out. 'They told him he could lose many of his abilities if they didn't treat it immediately. He could not believe it. He demanded a second opinion, so they called in Shubham—another relative of the CM. Completely clueless about medicine, but somehow held a position in the hospital thanks to his connections. I doubt he even sat for any medical exams himself. Anyway, this guy simply nodded along to what the others were saying. So, they prepared the guy for surgery.'

'What kind of surgery did the guys perform?'

'Nothing,' Ankit grinned. 'Just the pre-surgery procedure. While the guy was lying on the examination table, they served him a carbonated drink, which took care of the gas while he was passed out. When he woke up, he was told the "surgery" was successful and that he could leave. He went home and checked for scars. Want to guess what he found?'

'What?' Pooja asked, chuckling at the absurdity.

'Johnny had put a sticker on him. One that spelt out "feigning".'

'Holy shit! They seriously did that? What did he do then?' Pooja clutched her stomach, doubling over in laughter.

'Surprisingly, nothing. He was furious, of course. Somehow, he got hold of that trainee's number and called him later, using the most "sweetest, polite language", but never took any action. Last I heard, he had wormed his way into some minor position in the cabinet. I think the Carpet Ministry. You might have heard his name—Ravikant Goyal.'

'Oh my God! He was in the news recently—allegedly harassed a student at the Yale Parliamentary Exchange Programme... Johnny got him good, but wasn't he afraid of what that guy might do in retaliation?'

Unfinished Juxtaposition

'That man lives without a single thought about consequences.'

'Damn. It's crazy. Would you pull something like that?' Pooja asked.

'Hard to say. I never got an opportunity like that. Who knows? Maybe I would have. Maybe not. But now that I am likely shifting to the States, chances are almost zero.'

'Oh right, how was your interview?'

'It went well, but I know I could have done much better. The technical round was decent, I suppose, and Dr Jindal says that's the decisive factor. Apparently, the final decision is made by an algorithm, which heavily weighs technical round performance. I do have a couple more interviews lined up as backup. Let's see.'

'Dr Jindal already told you about the algo? He's an interesting character, full of random information. I like him. I remember this one time he was supposed to deliver a lecture on a new anaesthesia method, but instead, he spent 25 minutes talking about Julius Caesar and Cleopatra.'

'That does sound exactly like him,' Ankit said with a laugh, and Pooja joined in.

'All the best for your other interviews,' Pooja said. 'By the way, dinner? I'm famished,' she added, pointing towards a diner down the block.

Engrossed in conversation, they hadn't even realized when they had wandered out of the posh uptown residency and into the bustling city centre alive with people, colours and lights.

Pooja glanced at Ankit expectantly, as if daring him to confirm the spark they both felt.

'Sure. I think I know exactly what you'd like. How about momo with spicy chutney?'

Pooja blinked in surprise. She had not expected that. But the fact he remembered, touched her. 'Oh, you made me remember that! Here in the States, they call them dumplings. And they eat them with dips, not chutney.'

'Fancy!' Ankit said, rolling his eyes playfully as they stepped into a Chinese diner together.

9

Siberian Cranes

Dr Jindal's House

'Have you heard of Dr Joseph Carpue?' asked Dr Jindal.

It was Ankit's last night in the States, and Dr Jindal had invited him over for dinner one final time. They sat in his lounge, deep in conversation—discussing his interviews, the healthcare system in the US and, as always, random facts and trivia associated with medical care.

'I think I've heard the name.'

'He's a British doctor, credited with performing the first plastic surgery in 1816, which later came to be known as the Carpue Operation. He learnt the technique from an Indian potter.'

'Really?' Ankit raised an eyebrow, sceptical.

Dr Jindal nodded. 'As the story goes, an Indian bullock cart driver working for the British East India Company was captured by Tipu Sultan and his nose was cut as a mark of humiliation. He refused to be attended by a British doctor and instead chose a local healer from his village—a part-time physician who was also a potter named Kumar.

'Kumar peeled some skin from the man's forehead

and stitched it on to his nose. The nose grew back, as did the forehead skin. A British doctor who witnessed this wrote a detailed report, published it in a British medical journal and even attached a sketch of that cart driver. When Dr Carpue read that report, he was so intrigued that he came to India and spent years with that potter, learning the technique. In 1816, he went back to Britain and performed the same procedure himself.'

Ankit sat back, astonished. 'That is crazy! How did Kumar learn the technique?'

'It was wisdom passed down from generations—from father to son. A physician named Sushruta wrote about this technique in the book *Sushruta Samhita* some 2,500 years ago. And yet, we call Carpue the "Father of Plastic Surgery".'

'No doubt we Indians are so obsessed with *naak* (nose); we performed the first rhinoplasty in the world. But in the end, isn't medicine just a collective human effort? Every civilization has contributed in its own way.'

Dr Jindal leaned back in his chair, his gaze drifting towards the window where the last light of the setting sun could be seen. 'You know,' he began, his voice calm but tinged with a certain heaviness. 'It's fascinating how we, as humans, started as some of the weakest creatures in the animal kingdom. And yet, through intellect and science, we've risen to become the most powerful. That's an extraordinary story, isn't it? But here's the thing—we get so lost in the trivialities. Boundaries. Identities. Titles. None of it truly matters. At the end of the day, we're all part of the same species, striving for the same thing—a better life, health and progress.'

He paused and traced the rim of his coffee cup with his fingers. 'It's humbling when you think about it—how far we've come, the distance we've travelled. But instead of celebrating that, we chase illusions of perfection. We keep running towards some imaginary pinnacle that doesn't even exist. It's a mirage we've built for ourselves.' A small, reflective smile touched his lips. 'But maybe that's the point—to keep moving forward. Not for the illusion of greatness, but for the simple act of progress itself, to do the best we can. In that sense, I would say that humans, in a way, are prosthetic gods.'

'What does it mean?' Ankit asked with a blank expression.

'You might say that many things are destined—that we are shaped by the forces of fate. But at the same time, we have the power to shape our path. We have choices. We can steer ourselves in whatever direction we desire,' Dr Jindal explained. 'You, for example—you're striving for postgraduate training. You want to be one of the best, to be celebrated as a phenomenal doctor. That's admirable. But here's the thing: there's more to life than that. Don't fall into the trap of thinking that this is the end goal, and that everything you want is wrapped up in that next achievement. The truth is, the real game starts now. This is just the beginning. Think about it.'

Ankit exhaled, rubbing the back of his neck. 'I don't think I have ever looked at the big picture, Dr Jindal. Just thinking about it feels overwhelming. I've always focused on the next step, next plan of action—that is how I have pulled myself through. Wouldn't it be better to take it one day at a time? Plan the next goal when we get to that bridge?'

'Maybe. But for now, you can't just depend on the interviews. Have you thought of a Plan B, young man?'

Ankit hesitated. 'No, Dr Jindal, I haven't,' he admitted finally. 'All my interviews have gone well so far, and I'm confident of getting selected for residency in at least one hospital. But worst-case scenario, if things don't work out, I suppose I'll continue working at my current hospital in India. I don't think I have many options here.'

Dr Jindal studied him for a moment, then leaned forward slightly. 'You can appear for UCAT—it's the medical entrance exam for the UK. From what I have heard, it's relatively straightforward to get into the system, but there is a bottleneck as you advance in your career. They have surreptitiously created mid-level positions, overwhelmingly filled by immigrant physicians. And often, eligibility for an official training position is left to the discretion of a select few—a subtle violation of the principles of equal opportunities. But it's up to you whether to take it or leave it,' he said.

'It's interesting how discrimination here is so…polite. Back home, bigotry is out in the open; it takes time to recognize how disparities can be wrapped in charm,' Ankit said, smirking.

'All unchallenged prejudices lead to systemic stereotyping, which then manifests as discrimination and eventually pulls society backwards. So, it's important to stick your neck out and speak up—politely, but firmly,' Dr Jindal replied.

After a brief pause, he asked, 'What time do you leave tomorrow?'

'My flight is at 10 in the morning, so I'll leave for the airport by 6 a.m. Should take me about an hour to get there.'

'And you're sure you don't want us there to see you off?'

Ankit smiled, touched by the offer. 'Yes, Dr Jindal, really—it's too early, and I don't want to trouble you. Don't worry, I have already booked a cab; I'll manage.'

He was overwhelmed by the affection he had received from the old couple in the last few days. There was a certain kind of bond that formed between strangers of the same nationality in foreign lands—an unspoken solidarity, an invisible thread tying them together.

'All right then. Did you say goodbye to Dr Pooja?' Dr Jindal asked with a knowing look.

Like an observant relative, Dr Jindal had noticed when Ankit left with Pooja at his Diwali party and had inquired about it soon after. He had been delighted when Ankit recounted their old connection and their unexpected reunion.

Ankit nodded. 'We had lunch together this afternoon. I bid her farewell.'

It hadn't gone as well as he had hoped. Over the past few days, he and Pooja had met several times, growing closer with each meeting, and now, saying goodbye felt strangely heavy. There was an unspoken sadness between them, a quiet ache that neither had expected.

Amidst all the glitz and frenzy of this world, Ankit felt a deeper longing for human connection. Beneath the polished surface of Western individualism lay an invisible void—one that many seemed to accept but few acknowledged. He was reminded of what Freud had once called 'ordinary everyday unhappiness'—a quiet, persistent melancholy with no real remedy.

A knock at the door at 5.30 a.m. stopped Ankit in his tracks as he got ready to leave for his flight. He opened the door to find Dr Jindal standing outside, Mrs Jindal beside him, lunchbox in hand.

'You really thought we'd let you leave without seeing you off?' Dr Jindal said with a grin. 'Mrs Jindal insisted not only on dropping you at the airport but also on making you her famous corn-pepper sandwiches for the journey.'

Ankit swallowed, overwhelmed. 'Sir, Ma'am... I don't know what to say.'

Mrs Jindal patted his arm. 'There's nothing to say, dear. Just get dressed quickly; we have a flight to catch.'

Like many women who had followed their husbands to foreign lands in search of a better life, Mrs Jindal had once been filled with dreams. But over time, loneliness had settled in—a quiet, persistent ache hidden beneath the surface of her picture-perfect world. Seven-bedroom houses, expensive cars, glittering social events... None of it could fill the void of being adrift in a culture that was never truly hers.

At the airport, as she bid Ankit farewell, something in Ankit reminded her of a life she had once known, a life she had left behind in search of something new. The patterns of his clothes, the familiar scent of the air, the way he moved—everything about him felt like a thread back to her past. And in that moment, with an unexpected surge of courage, she stepped forward.

'I've been meaning to tell you,' she said softly, as if speaking to someone she had known for years. 'It's been so nice having you here. I wish you get the position you wanted. Then maybe we can see more of you.'

She hesitated, swallowing hard as the words she had buried for so long bubbled to the surface. 'We had a son... Someone like you. He's no longer with us,' she whispered, her eyes welling with unshed tears. 'When I see you, it brings everything back. I hope you understand.'

Ankit stood frozen, the weight of her words pressing down on him. He had no idea what to say. All he could do was look into her eyes and feel the pain there—a silent scream hidden beneath her calm façade.

Mrs Jindal, her tears now flowing freely, continued, 'If Rohit were alive, he would have been your age.'

Dr Jindal, who had been standing beside her, exhaled deeply. 'When I look back, I realize how lucky I was that nothing came easy for me. The whole path, as I look at it, was meaningful—the struggle gave me a sense of purpose. But Rohit... He had everything. I should never have given him so much without making him earn it.

Everything became mundane and meaningless to him. He lost his life to alcohol... And then we lost him. If I had a time machine, I would choose a simpler life—one that kept his hunger, his motivation going. That is something I will never forgive myself for.'

Ankit looked between them, the weight of their sorrow pressing down on him.

For all their wisdom, their success, their seemingly perfect lives—grief had left a wound that would never heal. And in that moment, he saw them not as mentors, not as elders, but simply as parents who had lost a child.

The glossy veneer of their life cracked wide open, revealing a quiet devastation beneath. And Ankit couldn't help but wonder—*how much pain do we hide behind the lives we so carefully construct?*

∞

10
Tolerating Ambiguity

Cafeteria, General Ward
Star Hospital, Jaigarh

'Dr Ankit?'

Ankit turned to see a young boy approaching him. 'Yes?'

'Hi, I'm Mahesh, Brijlal-ji's grandson. He said I should meet you—you'd help me find accommodation.'

'Oh yes! Here are my keys. And this is the landlord's number if you run into any issues. I'll pick up my stuff tomorrow morning if that's okay with you; I have a late shift today.'

'No problem, Dr Ankit. Thanks a ton.'

'You're giving him your room? Where will you live? And who is he?' Dr Rishabh, Ankit's colleague who had been watching the exchange, asked.

Ankit pocketed his hands. 'Brijlal-ji is our elderly neighbour back home in Palamgarh. Mahesh is his grandson—just moved here for his studies. Since I'm vacating my room anyway, I talked to the landlord and set him up,' he explained.

'Why are you vacating your room?'

'Oh, I'm going back to Palamgarh. I got my acceptance letter for the training programme in the States. I have already handed in my resignation to the hospital management.'

'And when were you going to tell us? You sly bastard! Running away without giving a party. Congratulations, man! Wow!' Dr Rishabh clapped Ankit hard on the back. 'How can you go about with that poker face? If I got selected, I'd be grinning for months.'

Hearing the commotion, a few more colleagues gathered around.

'What's going on?'

'Ankit's been accepted for training in the US!'

A chorus of congratulations erupted.

'Wow, man, big news. Where did you get accepted?' someone asked.

'It's a combined surgery and oncology programme at Northbridge General Hospital. I'll be training under Dr Anita Silva.'

A low whistle. 'Damn, that's the Mecca of surgical training.'

'Yeah, I'm pretty excited about it,' Ankit replied.

Dr Rishabh raised an eyebrow. 'Pretty excited? No offence, bro, but you look like someone stole your lunch. Why the long face? Are you not happy?'

Ankit hesitated. 'I am happy, bro. It's just…sometimes success doesn't feel like success when it comes too late.' A brief silence followed before he continued, shaking off the moment. 'Anyway, I'm off to Palamgarh tomorrow. I have applied for the visa and will hopefully receive it in a week or so. My flight is next month.'

'Are you sure your visa will be approved?' another colleague asked. 'I mean, there are rumours that doctors are struggling to get their training visas. Something about the new visa policy…'

'Those are just rumours,' Ankit shrugged off the comment. 'Look, healthcare is always top priority—like it or not. Countries like the US have stringent immigration policies, yes, but they've always welcomed professionals in STEM fields. What's really been happening is a crackdown on low-wage migrants—there's been public outrage about locals losing their jobs, so the system's tightening up on people exploiting family-based immigration routes. But for healthcare scholars and physicians? There's never been, and probably never will be, any real roadblocks, given the huge demand. Hopefully, my visa will come through soon. Fingers crossed.'

11

JEDI Stands For Justice, Equity, Diversity and Inclusion

Terminal 2
Singh International Airport, Palamgarh

'ALICIA BERENSON WAS THIRTY-THREE YEARS OLD WHEN SHE KILLED HER HUSBAND.'

What a lovely first sentence, Ankit thought as he read through *The Silent Patient*, the novel he'd brought for the flight. Pooja had highly recommended it.

They had exchanged numbers at the Diwali party, and when she heard about his acceptance, she had been ecstatic. Why, though, he didn't quite understand. Or maybe he did, but didn't want to dwell on the possibility.

'Oh, I've read this one. What a thriller.'

The voice came from his right. Ankit turned to see a young South Indian man, probably in his 20s, seated next to him. The last time he had chatted with his co-passenger had been with Dr Jindal. Aside from making a few friends, he had run into his ex as well after that. *Maybe talking to your co-passengers is a good thing.*

'Yeah, I've heard great reviews, and it has a fantastic opening line.' He paused before adding, 'Hi, I'm Ankit.'

'Hi, I'm Swami. I loved this book, man. Do you want to hear another really interesting opening line? I read it this morning in the unlikeliest of places—a physics book,' the guy chattered on.

'I'm intrigued. What is it?' Ankit asked.

'Wait, I have got it here.' He shuffled through his bag and pulled out a book, flipping it open.

'*States of Matter* by David Goodstein. Listen to this: Ludwig Boltzmann, who spent much of his life studying statistical mechanics, died in 1906, by his own hand. Paul Ehrenfest, carrying on the work, died similarly in 1933. Now it is our turn to study statistical mechanics. Perhaps it will be wise to approach the subject cautiously.'

Ankit let out a laugh. 'That's dark but funny. Are you preparing for some competitive exams?'

'Oh no, I just read it for fun,' Swami said, a little too quickly, his voice too casual.

Ankit gave him a knowing look. 'What type of guy reads physics for fun? What do you do?'

Swami shifted in his seat, suddenly feeling warm, the space around him shrinking. 'Oh, I am a student. Automobile Engineering, Bombay Technical University. Got selected for a summer internship at Ford Motors in Detroit. What do you do?' he asked, his voice sounding strange to his own ears.

'Damn impressive, kid. I'm a doctor—joining my residency training.'

'Oh, that's pretty cool,' Swami responded, his

mouth feeling dry. The words felt awkward, like they weren't really his. He tried to swallow but his throat felt tight.

For a moment, silence settled between them. Ankit returned to his book, and Swami did his best to settle back into his seat. But it was difficult. The hum of the engines seemed louder than usual, pressing into his ears. The air in the cabin felt thick, stifling. He glanced out of the window—the horizon distant, unreachable.

Flying had never been his favourite thing. He had travelled by plane only a few times, and turbulence—whether mid-air or during take-off and landing—always left him uneasy. Now, as the aircraft began to ascend, he gripped the armrest tightly, his fingers pressing into the leather.

It's fine. Just a normal flight.

His heart wasn't convinced. His chest felt tight, his breath shallow. He tried to distract himself by watching the flight attendants preparing the food trays, but even their movements felt exaggerated, like everything was happening in slow motion. His head felt heavy, and the chatter of the other passengers became almost too much to bear.

When the air hostesses started rolling out lunch trays, Swami's voice came out sharper than intended. 'I think I'll just have water for now,' he said quickly, hoping he wouldn't have to face the food. His stomach was already churning.

Ankit glanced at him but didn't comment.

Seeing Ankit looking at him, Swami spoke up again.

'What will you have for lunch? I've heard Indian Air serves excellent chicken cutlets.'

'No, I don't eat meat. It's sambhar idli for me,' Ankit replied.

A grin broke across Swami's face. 'You can thank us Tamil folks for that. I'm from Thanjavur, the place where sambhar actually originated.'

'Really?'

'Yes! The story goes that when Sambhaji, the son of the great Shivaji, visited his uncle—the king of Thanjavur—a great feast was held in his honour. Sambhaji was not fond of kokum, which is one of the main ingredients in Tamil cuisine, so the royal chef improvised. He replaced kokum with tamarind and curry leaves in one of the lentil dishes. The result was a fusion so well received by everyone there that they named it "Sambhar" after him,' Swami said proudly.

'Interesting. You are full of random trivia—you remind me of someone,' Ankit replied, thinking about his encounter with Dr Jindal.

'I love history and trivia. By the way, do you know how this thing works?' Swami pointed at the in-flight entertainment system. 'I've been trying for 45 minutes; think it's broken.'

'You need to press that red button.'

'I did. Nothing.'

'Hmm. Might actually be broken. You should call the attendant,' Ankit suggested.

'It's fine, leave it. I'll just listen to some podcast on my phone.'

'You paid for the ticket—and all the amenities. If something's broken, you should ask for it to be fixed or replaced,' Ankit said, unwilling to let the issue slide.

'I see your point, but…it's okay, really,' Swami replied, hesitating.

'If you say so.'

∞

Ankit was engrossed in his novel. Alicia had not only murdered her husband but had also chosen to remain mute throughout her trial. The mystery drew him in, but a small chime broke his focus. He looked up and realized he'd been reading for nearly an hour without stopping.

He watched as an attendant hurried over to the passenger who had called for assistance.

'Hey, I think my entertainment system's broken,' the man complained, his voice heavy with an accent. Judging by his looks, Ankit guessed he was American.

After a few minutes of fiddling, the attendant accepted defeat. 'Yes, sir, it seems there's a problem. I'm really sorry. Just give me two minutes; I'll sort it out right away.'

She returned to her station, spoke to her senior, then came back—this time with company.

'Sir, we sincerely apologize for this inconvenience. We'd like to move you to business class. Please follow my colleague,' the senior attendant said. 'As a gesture of goodwill, your aviation points for this flight will be doubled.'

Ankit looked on, impressed but also puzzled. *Is it*

because he's white, or has Indian Air really upped its customer service game?

He glanced at Swami, who was absorbed in his phone, his earphones on, and nudged him.

'See that guy getting up? He had a faulty entertainment system and complained about it. Guess what? He got moved to business class,' Ankit informed Swami.

It took 10 more minutes of coaxing before Swami finally agreed to speak up. When the attendant arrived, another five minutes had passed.

'Ma'am, if it's not much of a bother, would you mind checking the entertainment system? It seems to be broken,' Swami said politely.

She fiddled with it briefly, then turned to Swami with a not-so-subtle frown on her face. 'Are you planning to use this system, sir?' she asked.

'I can't; it doesn't work. Could you please help?'

'Sorry, sir, there's nothing I can do. I could offer you some magazines if you like?' she replied.

'No thanks, it's okay,' Swami said meekly.

'Will that be all, sir?'

'Yes, thank you.'

The attendant walked away briskly.

Ankit stared after her, fuming in disbelief. 'Why didn't you say anything? This is ridiculous!' he exclaimed.

'It's fine; don't worry. Maybe that guy got special treatment because he's a foreigner. We treat guests like gods in India, right?'

'Sure—but that doesn't mean treating your own people unfairly. You paid for the same services. They owe you the same standard of treatment.'

As Ankit pressed the call button, the same attendant came over.

'Yes, sir, how can I help you?' she asked.

'I'd like to lodge a complaint against you and the airline, madam, for biased service. A few minutes ago, a passenger with a faulty entertainment system was moved to business class and offered bonus points. When my co-passenger here reported the exact same issue, your response was highly unprofessional and dismissive. This feels like racial bias. If that's how your airline treats its own people, I'll be raising this publicly, on social media and elsewhere.'

The attendant blanched slightly. 'Sir, I am really sorry. There must be some misunderstanding. Please allow me a minute.'

'I saw what I saw. I don't believe there has been any misunderstanding.'

She returned minutes later with her senior. The tone had changed. 'Sirs, we deeply regret the oversight. We'd like to offer you both an upgrade to business class, with double points, and complimentary dessert as an apology.'

Swami and Ankit quietly collected their belongings and followed the attendant.

Once settled in their plush new seats, Swami looked over and smiled at Ankit. 'That was epic! The bravest thing I've seen in a long time,' he exclaimed.

'There's nothing heroic about it,' Ankit replied calmly. 'It's just about realizing your worth and asking for what is rightfully yours. I don't blame you for pushing back—colonization filled us with a twisted sense of inadequacy. Did you know that by the time the British left India in 1947, our share of the global economy had dropped from 25 per cent to just 4 per cent? But even that wasn't our biggest loss. What we really lost was our self-respect, our pride.'

Swami nodded slowly, processing. 'Now that you put it that way, it does make sense. It is like...imposter syndrome, right? That feeling of not belonging, not being good enough—even when you are...'

Ankit's hands trembled slightly as he replied, the emotion of the moment weighing on him. 'Swami, I know this might seem like making a big deal out of a small issue, but the world is not just broken because of bad people; it's also because good people don't speak up.

'You know about the bystander effect, right? When people see something wrong and stay silent, thinking someone else will step in? That silence—that inaction—lets injustice grow. And it doesn't just happen in public. It happens in our homes, our classrooms, our offices.'

Swami fidgeted with the hem of his shirt, eyes fixed ahead. He wanted to respond, but the words felt jammed somewhere between his throat and chest.

'Even someone like you,' Ankit continued gently, 'someone dynamic and smart, carries a little voice in the back of your mind that tells you that you don't deserve certain things. And it's not just you, it's all of us. That voice is not ours—it was planted there. When we settle for less, it's because we have been taught not to expect more.'

Swami's mouth felt dry. He opened it to speak but his

words faltered. 'I...uh... I mean, I don't know. Maybe it's not that simple,' he said finally, his voice trailing off. He turned to the window, hoping the sky outside would offer some clarity. His heart beat a little faster as he realized he couldn't quite articulate what he wanted to say.

Ankit, seemingly undeterred, pressed on. 'I get it. It's never simple. It's caste, class, race, creed, gender—every identity we carry comes with baggage we didn't ask for. And slowly, it becomes the lens through which we see the world—and ourselves. The silos, the profiling, the unconscious bias...it shrinks our idea of who we are allowed to be.'

There was a long pause. The quiet in the business-class cabin seemed deeper somehow—more insulated.

'I've been through it too,' Ankit said, his voice softer now. 'And honestly? It makes me anxious, Swami. I'm heading to a new country to pursue my goals, my education, my dreams, but I don't know if the system there will support me or push back. I wonder if I'll have to fight harder just to stand where others are welcomed. I just want you to understand where I'm coming from.'

Swami's fingers curled slightly around the edge of the seat. He swallowed hard, still unsure how to respond. 'I...I mean, yeah... I understand,' he said, his voice barely above a whisper. 'It's just...it's all so complicated, you know?'

He glanced up at Ankit for a moment, then quickly looked away, feeling an unfamiliar tension rise in his chest. He wanted to say more, to ask questions, but was overwhelmed by the flood of thoughts he didn't yet have the words to name.

12

Status Quo

Dr Silva's Office
Northbridge General Hospital

Dr Silva's large office felt both professional and cosy. Her big mahogany desk was neatly arranged with files and papers. Sunlight streamed through thick curtains, bathing the room in a gentle warmth. Certificates and awards lined the walls, showcasing her achievements in the field of oncology.

A knock at the door made her look up. Dr Gray and Dr Hawker stood in front of her, their expressions a mix of gratitude and cautious optimism.

'How can I help you, doctors?' Dr Silva asked, her voice betraying measured curiosity.

She was mildly surprised to see both the Dean and the Director of Education in her office. As she observed the two men before her, their differences were striking. Dr Hawker, a short man with a stocky build, sank into the chair with an almost apologetic posture. Dr Gray, in contrast, was a handsome man in his mid-50s. His salt-and-pepper hair was styled in a flawless Ivy League cut and his muscular frame—especially his chest and forearms—hinted at regular visits to the gym.

'Dr Silva, I just wanted to thank you for making time for Mr Kapoor this week,' Dr Gray began. 'I was with Dr Hawker, going through the shortlisted candidates for the residency programme, and we happened to walk past your office. So I thought I'd drop in, thank you in person and hand over the final list for the Oncology Residency. You've got four new members on your team, two of whom are international graduates.'

'Oh yes, I remember interviewing one of them myself—Dr Ankit,' the dean chimed in. 'What a brilliant chap! I'm sure you'll like him, Dr Silva.'

But beneath the surface pleasantries, both men were eager to address a deeper rift—one that had lingered since an incident the previous year.

Back then, Dr Silva had drawn a hard line. Frustrated by the declining quality of her trainees, she submitted a formal report to the national selection board, which triggered an inquiry and led to a substantial fine for the institution. The fallout had been severe. Dr Hawker, who had been heading recruitment at the time, felt publicly humiliated. Ever since, a quiet tension had lingered between them and Dr Silva.

But Dr Silva maintained her uncompromising stance. In her world of surgical oncology, there was no space for mediocrity. Every decision, every move had life-or-death consequences. She wasn't just looking for competence; she demanded integrity. To her, integrity meant doing the right thing even when no one was watching. That standard wasn't negotiable.

She had made her expectations crystal clear. Legacy candidates and those padded with glowing recommendations didn't impress her. She wanted grit. Genuine commitment. A willingness to go above and beyond the checklist and truly honour the gravity of the profession. Her trainees who faltered were placed on a remediation plan, and if they continued to fall short, she didn't hesitate to suggest a change in specialty—or even profession.

When Dr Silva didn't immediately respond, Dr Gray leaned back slightly, his fingers tapping gently on the edge of her desk. 'This time, during the interviews, I was searching for something more,' he began, his tone thoughtful. 'It's not that there are set rules for this sort of thing—so much of it relies on instinct, assumptions, even unconscious bias. But I tried to let all that go. I wanted to see beyond the numbers, beyond the pristine CV and perfect test scores. In healthcare, we need more than technical competence. We need people who still see the human being behind the illness, who can bring compassion into a field where it's so easy to lose sight of why we're here.'

He paused, his gaze resting on Dr Silva, who stayed silent. 'You see, without that humanity, our profession risks becoming a machine—cold, transactional, handed over to big pharma, politicians and bureaucracies. And with all the noise—the media hysteria, the system pressure—it's hard to stay grounded and easy to forget why we do what we do. But it's essential. That's why I was deliberate about who we bring in this time around.'

Dr Silva tilted her head, intrigued.

Dr Gray pressed on. 'Ankit stood out to me—not just for being smart, though he obviously is. Coming from where he does, you expect him to know his numbers, to excel under pressure. But it wasn't his technical skills that struck me. It was his understanding of ethics, of humanity. I gave him a hypothetical scenario—an undocumented patient, no insurance, facing pressure to leave the hospital for reasons that had nothing to do with their care. And his response? It wasn't simplistic or overly idealistic. It wasn't emotional. It was thoughtful, balanced. He talked about communication, finding resources and advocating for what's right without alienating those around him. That's what I was looking for.'

Dr Silva nodded slowly, a flicker of interest in her eyes.

'He also spoke about medical education, about reform. Not in a loud, revolutionary way—but in quiet, meaningful steps. Change from within. Protecting what's sacred in this field. That kind of vision is rare, and frankly, it's exactly what we need.'

Dr Silva leaned forward slightly. 'It sounds like you're thinking beyond recruitment, Dr Gray. You're setting a precedent.'

Dr Gray smiled faintly. 'I hope so. We can't afford to keep approaching this process the way we always have. The future of healthcare depends on who we bring into it. And if we don't adapt, we risk losing everything we've worked so hard to build.'

Dr Silva exhaled, clearly impressed, though her mind was already elsewhere. 'You've given me a lot to think about,' she said softly. 'And speaking of new perspectives, I have got a clinical case discussion with Mr Kapoor later. Something tells me there's more to explore there,' she added.

Dr Gray's smile widened, a knowing look in his eyes. 'I think you'll find it enlightening. Let me know how it goes.'

'Well, thank you, Dr Gray, and thank you, Dr Hawker. It was no trouble fitting Mr Kapoor into the schedule—I just had to shuffle a few patients and drop a couple. As for the new recruits, I'm looking forward to working with them. If they're as good as you say, Dr Hawker, I'll take your word for it.' She then shifted her attention to Dr Gray. 'How do you know Mr Kapoor, by the way?'

'Oh, he's a friend of an old friend. We've crossed paths a few times over the years,' he replied.

Dr Silva gave a polite nod. 'All right. Will that be all, gentlemen?' She had little patience for small talk—what she once considered polite conversation now felt like a tax on her time.

Dr Hawker cleared his throat. 'There's one more tiny matter. Over the last few years, you've declined some of the residency recruits. We would like to avoid that this year.'

'Dr Hawker, you know how much I value efficiency and integrity in my team. If the recruits you hand me are not up to the mark, I'll have no choice but to decline them. Is that why I have two international doctors this year?'

'No, it was the algorithm. We just happened to accept more diverse applications. And more from other ethnicities as well.'

'Any reason for that, Dr Hawker?' she asked pointedly.

'Well, there was an article—'

'I persuaded him,' Dr Gray interrupted smoothly, flashing his boyish smile. 'To cast a wider net this year. Accept applications from everywhere, then choose the best. Merit is still the guiding light—but the pool should reflect the real world.'

He cleared his throat, breaking the silence that had stretched a beat too long as Dr Silva looked at them, her eyes narrowed—alert, but unreadable. 'Dr Silva,' he began, his voice measured, 'we have implemented quite a few changes this year. We've overhauled our selection process. It's far more transparent now. For instance, during interviews, we take deliberate steps to reduce unconscious bias. Candidate names and identifying details are removed prior to panel review, and interviewers do not receive CVs. They're expected to evaluate applicants solely on non-identifiable information and qualitative impressions.'

He paused, then continued. 'We've also moved away from relying on high-profile recommendations or superficial metrics. Instead, we're focusing on objective reviews—assessing long-term potential and values. And it goes both ways—residents evaluate us, too. That feedback loop creates mutual accountability and, we hope, a more compassionate, inclusive workforce.'

Dr Hawker, who'd been nodding along, added, 'We know we can't undo the frustrations of the past, but we want you to know we've taken your concerns seriously. Your programme is the crown jewel of this institution, and we're doing everything in our power to ensure you get the kind of recruits who meet your standards.'

Dr Silva leaned back in her chair, her expression softening slightly. 'I appreciate the effort,' she said, her voice steady and her resolve clear. 'I understand these things take time, but the bar remains high. If trainees can't meet the expectations, I will hold them accountable. This programme isn't just about producing doctors—it's about producing the best doctors, the ones who can take this field forward.'

Dr Gray nodded, his eyes shining with a flicker of admiration. 'We wouldn't expect anything less from you, Dr Silva.'

Dr Hawker offered a small, relieved smile. 'We'll keep you updated as the changes take shape. Thank you for your patience and your standards. They keep this programme at the forefront.'

As they left her office, Dr Silva watched them go, their words lingering in her mind. While she appreciated their effort, she knew time and results would be the ultimate proof. For now, she was content to let the conversation close one chapter, even as another began.

13

Reconciling with the Past

The Waterline Lounge

'Hey, I'm so sorry; I am late. First, there was the traffic, and then it took forever to find the location—but I must say it's worth it. This place looks great,' Pooja said, slightly out of breath.

'I love the ambiance too,' Ankit replied, getting up to pull out a chair for her.

'So…' she said as she settled in, 'What did you do while waiting?'

'You know, I was just sitting here thinking… and something crossed my mind. We've never really talked about this, but I'd like to share it with you. Do you want to hear it?'

'Why not?'

'When we were in medical school, everything was so curated—so tightly structured—that it did not allow us the space to "think". I mean really *think*, to ask questions, to explore. With such a narrow lane of career choices, entering medicine felt like scoring a self-goal towards a mirage—or an illusion, to be more precise. I have been dreaming all these years… And only now do I feel like

I am beginning to wake up. Like I am finally using my own mind.' He looked out the window briefly, then back at her. 'Do you remember Ajay? We used to call him AJ; he was like a rock star.'

'Yes,' Pooja said with a soft smile. 'Everyone had a crush on him. What is he up to now?'

'He passed away—a massive MI. About a year ago. He was overworked.' He paused. 'I still can't get over it. He used to be so active on social media—always posting updates about his life… Then one day, he was just gone… forever. Obviously, there is more to it than just a heart attack, but… He is gone now,' Ankit continued quietly. 'It's the lived experience that teaches you more. What I learnt from AJ is to stay balanced; it's not always about productivity.'

Ankit took a deep breath. 'When AJ passed, Pooja… I cannot even begin to describe the shock. It hit me like a wave. Two days before it happened, we had worked a shift together. Everything was normal. We laughed, talked and then went our separate ways. And then…the news came, and I could not believe it. It felt impossible, like the world had tilted off its axis.'

Pooja reached for his hand instinctively. 'Death is bewildering for the ones left behind. A living, breathing person gets reduced to a body. And the rest of us, the ones left behind… We are expected to move on, carry on with life, as if nothing happened. I am so sorry you had to go through that,' she said. What she actually wanted to say was, 'I am sorry I wasn't with you.' But the words stuck in her throat.

'I went to his house, still in disbelief, thinking maybe it was a mistake. But then I saw his family. His mother hugged me, sobbing uncontrollably. She kept asking, "What was this all about? What was the point?" Her words—Pooja, they have haunted me ever since. Standing there, seeing their grief, looking at AJ—lifeless, cold—everything I had been striving for my whole life suddenly seemed pointless.'

Pooja held his hand tighter, noticing the way his eyes flickered, as if reliving it all.

'All my life, I have been running. Competing. Trying to prove myself. For milestones—money, status, luxury cars, international trips. But in that moment, it all felt hollow. I realized I had been chasing things that might not even matter in the end.' His voice trembled slightly, but he pressed on. 'Seeing AJ like that changed me, Pooja. It was not just a wake-up call—it shook me to my very core. Made me question everything. And that is terrifying. It is like standing at the edge of a cliff, looking down at everything you have built, realizing it might not be solid ground.'

Pooja remained silent, her expression tender, eyes brimming with empathy. 'For months, I pulled away from everyone. I needed to understand what it all meant. I missed AJ deeply. But strangely, even in his absence, he taught me something. That life is not about milestones. It is about being alive. Right here. Right now.

'It's hard. I still struggle with it... But I am learning to let go of the constant need to achieve, to prove something. I am learning to embrace life's messiness, accept its contradictions. Because that is where the meaning lies—not in the trophies or the accolades, but in the connections. In the fleeting moments that remind us we are alive.'

Ankit's voice wavered slightly, but he held Pooja's gaze. 'And AJ... He taught me that. In the most profound way.'

There was a silence between them—charged, gentle, deeply human.

Then Pooja spoke. 'For me, everything was about following the path—the one that was expected of me... Society and culture wrote my script. But then...my inner voice started whispering, "What about free will, darling?"

'I was young, intelligent, probably good-looking, and came from a privileged background. External success was the least expected of me. And it was so hard to be a contrarian. Ankit, you were always so wise—your clarity, even back then, was impressive. But...the class divide, the social cliques—it all made it so difficult to get close to people like you.'

She looked down briefly, then back up. 'And oh my God, the peer pressure! All my friends were into something more "hip"—more glamorous—than what our classmates had to offer; I got stuck in that trap. And just when I thought I was settling into something stable...one of my best buddies, Simla, died by suicide.'

Ankit's eyes widened and his face fell.

'She'd worked with me in the ICU for the last decade. We used to party almost every weekend; no one saw it coming. I am still shocked.' Pooja's voice broke slightly.

'Death is the ultimate truth,' Ankit said in a low, reflective tone. 'It's a reminder to live the unlived—so that when your time comes, you're ready. But everyone wants to live forever, even though our time here is limited.'

'I wish they had taught us this in the first year of medical school,' Pooja replied with a faint smile. 'I chased class, looks, sycophants and peer validation to steer my social life through med school and beyond. But here I am—internally hollow. It's like there's a deep vacuum inside me. I have everything I could wish for, yet the inner conflicts remain unresolved. They refuse to go away, like one of those "bop bags" that keep bouncing back.'

She paused, her voice growing quieter. 'Simla and I talked about this a few months ago… I have realized everyone is in the same boat. Life is the best equalizer, Ankit. Someone please help me get out of this rut—so I can be finally free.'

'There is a way, Ankit replied. 'The path is treacherous, savage, imperfect; it demands deep introspection and self-awareness. But it's the only path towards tranquillity—and it's the longest journey with no end.'

'Like never before, I am ready—without my prejudices, without the biases or fear of rejection. I may even ask for forgiveness—for not giving myself a chance to know you better. Time has debunked all my assumptions. In me, you will find a friend who intends to connect through vulnerability—not performance. Someone who will always put her best foot forward.'

There was a long silence, rich with things unsaid.

Then Ankit said softly, 'I completely understand; I find my solace when you say nothing at all.'

Pooja smiled, a warmth rising behind her eyes. 'Normally, I'd have told my best friends about coming to meet you, but today... It does not matter. I feel so happy, Ankit. Really happy. I shared my most vulnerable parts, like never before. And I know they came from my true self. I have never felt so light.'

'To be trusted ranks higher for me than being loved.'

Pooja laughed gently. 'All right Dr Ankit—enough of the soul-searching. Let's change the subject. Tell me, how's it going with you at Northbridge?'

'I love the place. I love the programme, the exposure I'm getting...and, most of all, our programme head; she's a genius. But more than that, it's the environment—where questions are encouraged, critical thinking is nurtured and ethics are central to research. I'm finally working with mentors whose papers and books I read in my initial years. Now, having real dialectical discussions with them, watching how they practise—not just the clinical skills, but the soft skills—it is like striking gold.

'Ooh, sounds like someone is in love with Dr Silva!' Pooja teased.

Ankit chuckled. 'Ha ha—no, no! You know what I mean. I'm learning so much from her; it's amazing. And this new regimen she developed? Brilliant! She's a genius mind, no doubt—but maybe not the most socially fluent person.'

'She can be a bit awkward sometimes,' Pooja agreed. 'But she's one of the most important minds here. At one point, she was a consultant to the previous POTUS.'

'Really? How did that go?'

'It went well… Till she made the First Lady wait over half an hour. The Secret Service went Rambo over her ass but pretty soon they realized who they were dealing with. They backed off. She is the perfect example of someone getting away with anything—because she's just that brilliant.'

'There are rumours she got away with skipping a disciplinary hearing against her. Is that true?'

'Absolutely. More than once. The administration won't touch her. No one wants to lose a doctor like her. From a business point of view, it's a no-brainer—she brings in one of the highest revenue shares. Celebrities, top athletes, high-ranking government officials and diplomats—you name it. And most of the issues against her? Ego clashes. Everyone knows she has reached the pinnacle of ethics, and her clinical outcomes speak for themselves.'

'I don't think I've met anyone as successful as—not just in medicine, but in any field,' Ankit said with admiration. 'The depth of knowledge, the finesse—it is exceptional. She's a perfect role model for the youth today.'

Pooja tilted her head. 'Success is subjective, Ankit. Dr Silva never married; if you were to ask a nosy aunt back home whether she thinks Dr Silva is successful, she'd probably say "no". Because for them, a woman is truly successful only when she settles down and has a family.'

Ankit raised an eyebrow. 'Ahem… I sense some personal behind that,' he said pointedly.

'Hmm,' Pooja sighed. 'As a divorcee with no kids, even here in the US, my relatives keep pestering me with their "concern". My aunt called today, trying to set me up with some 50-year-old widower in her husband's family. Apparently, I'm still of childbearing age and this will be my last chance. Anyway, jokes on them—my eggs are already safely frozen.'

'Wow, the opportunity of a lifetime, Dr Pooja. If I were you, I'd leave everything, run right back and fall into his arms.'

'Stop teasing me.' She paused and took in a deep, deliberate breath, as if preparing to share something from deep within. Her eyes reflected a storm of thoughts as she looked at Ankit. Her voice shifted, lower now, vulnerable.

'If you really want to know the truth, here it is. Growing up, I never had to worry about money. There was always bread on the table. But there were conditions, unspoken yet deeply ingrained. I internalized those expectations, and they shaped everything about me. And that is what conformity does. It doesn't just influence you; it traps you.'

'Civilization thrives on order and conventions,' Pooja continued, her voice steady but distant. 'But that order comes with immense human suffering. And for me, just being born a woman came with its own burdens. In different cultures, that alone can dictate your destiny—often without you even realizing it.'

She paused, eyes fixed on a point somewhere far beyond the room.

'As I grew older, I tried to take some control over my own life, to defy that order. The backlash was brutal. I was humiliated—psychologically, emotionally—gaslighted at every turn. There has always been this deep guilt, Ankit. Guilt that has followed me for decades. Even when I tried to break free, the trauma stayed; hidden, but always there. I do not carry insecurities about many things, but the mental tension, the constant pressure... It suffocates. And the loneliness—it is more than just being alone. It is the kind of loneliness where you have no one to share your innermost thoughts and feelings with.'

She looked at him then, the silence heavy between them.

'This world, the system, always told me not to be vulnerable. That vulnerability is weakness. But now I've learnt—the more vulnerable you are, the freer you become. What we think, what we feel... It is not unique. It is shared. It is human. But I didn't always see it that way. There was fear. Confusion. Layers and layers of it. I was caught in this vicious cycle—wanting to conform, yet yearning to break free.'

Her tone softened as she continued. 'Eventually, I began to enjoy my freedom. I stopped caring about what others thought. I decided I did not want anyone in my life who would bring back that same oppressive mindset—someone who would tell me what to do or how to live. And honestly, it is only recently that women—even in so-called developed societies—have started to truly take control of their lives. But for so many, the conditions haven't changed.'

She let out a quiet breath. 'So, yes, I enjoy my independence. But there are always these lingering questions: Do I want someone in my life as I grow older? Who could I possibly connect with? It is not about ticking boxes—status, money, looks. It is about finding someone who understands, who listens. Most conversations around me are about shopping, holidays, climbing some academic or social ladder. But what about the self? Where are the people who really think about who they are? That is who I want to find—someone I can share my thoughts with. Someone who feels like home.'

Ankit sat in silence, taken aback by her words. He felt her pain, her strength, and most of all, her courage. He struggled to find the right words, but his eyes reflected his admiration for the woman sitting in front of him. When he finally replied, his voice was heavy with the weight of sincerity. 'Pooja, this is incredible. This kind of discovery… It only comes from deep self-reflection and time. What you have shared is profound. I… I admire you for it.'

As he spoke, he leaned in closer, resting his hands on the table, his gaze steady. There was something in her story that resonated with him. In that moment, Ankit felt a connection that went beyond words—one rooted in vulnerability and the freedom that comes from embracing life's complexities. Feeling the need to shift the atmosphere again, Pooja ventured, 'Tell me, why didn't you get married? Did you date anyone?'

'Yeah, I did date someone. But it was a brief affair.'

'Woman or man?' she teased.

'Very funny.'

'So?'

'So?'

'Who did you date?'

'No one. I just wanted to see your reaction.'

'What? Why would you do that? Are you in some kind of hope, Ankit ji?' Pooja wagged her eyebrows.

'Look at me, Pooja. I'm 35, but thanks to my androgenetic baldness and emerging paunch, I look 45. After two residencies, here I am, starting over with a zero bank balance. I'm a lot of things—but hopeful is not one of them.'

'Okay, okay—don't get defensive. I was just kidding. How's Pari?' she asked, changing the subject to his niece.

'She's good. In fifth grade now. She will probably come to visit me with my Mum and Dad once her term ends. I'm thinking, if she likes it here, maybe she can stay on and do the rest of her schooling here.'

'That is a good idea; will your parents shift here?'

'No, I doubt it.'

'Will they leave Pari with you then? How will you care for her? You spend most of your day at the hospital!'

'I could hire a babysitter or a full-time babysitter. But yeah, it probably won't sit right with them; they will never agree.'

'They might, if there's a woman around... A motherly figure to care for her.'

'You mean a nanny?' Ankit asked, puzzled.

Pooja burst into laughter.

'No, you idiot.'
'Then?'
'Nothing,' she said, still smiling.

14

Identity Crisis

Conference Hall
Hotel Blue Lagoon

'Dr Aan-Khit?' The instructor squinted at the list, trying to sound out the name.

'It's Dr Ankit,' he corrected, his voice flat.

'Yeah, never mind. Here is your brochure and seat number. Please settle down quickly according to the seating arrangement—we're about to start,' the instructor said briskly, already moving on.

It was the Annual Ethics Seminar held by the Delphia Medical Association, a compulsory event attended by teams of doctors from every hospital in the region. Northbridge's team consisted of seven doctors, four of whom were international graduates, including Ankit.

Ankit reluctantly slid into a seat at the back of the conference room, his scepticism practically radiating off him. *What could an ethics class possibly teach me?* He had spent years mastering the most advanced healthcare technologies, collecting gold medals like participation trophies, topping every academic chart imaginable. He knew his field inside out—or so he believed. Ethics? That was just a checkbox. His conscience, he thought, already covered everything that mattered.

He crossed his arms and leaned back, exuding quiet resistance.

The instructor mispronouncing his name made his teeth grind. He clenched his jaw, suppressing a surge of irritation. It was not just the name—it was everything. Ankit had walked into the event carrying a suitcase full of assumptions. Ethics, he thought, was not a subject that demanded debate or deep thought. In all his training, it had always been relegated to a few forgettable textbook paragraphs, never meant for real-world application. So why was this course suddenly mandatory?

A whisper from a colleague pulled him from his thoughts. 'You know Dr Silva is strict about this class, right? She will not pass anyone who does not take it seriously, especially the internal assessment. You will need to score well and apply this stuff in clinical settings.'

Ankit raised an eyebrow, half-puzzled, half-irritated. Apply ethics in the real world? He found the notion laughable. 'Non-malfeasance. Beneficence,' he muttered. 'I have read the terms. Just words. I have never needed someone to explain them.'

The colleague leaned closer, dropping their voice lower. 'It is not about knowing the words. Ethics kicks in when medicine alone isn't enough. It is for the grey zones. When nothing is clear, and every option hurts.'

Ankit frowned but said nothing. The idea unsettled him. Could there be moments when all his knowledge, his brilliance, his precision might not be enough? He shook the thought away and scribbled meaninglessly in his notebook.

The instructor's tone grated on him: clipped, sharp, almost rude *Ethics is taught rudely*. The contradiction felt ironic.

Still, he stayed put. Maybe out of curiosity. Maybe out of obligation. But something kept Ankit seated. He'd meant to breeze through the session, check the box and move on to the real work, the kind that actually mattered—like his surgical oncology research. But a faint discomfort crept in. Something about the way the class was framed, the way his colleague had spoken—it stuck with him. *What if ethics was not fluff?* What if it did have a place in the pristine, black-and-white world he had so carefully built?

He adjusted the pen in his hand and tried to focus, wondering, for the first time, if the session might challenge him in ways he had not anticipated.

The instructor—a tightly wound man in his late 30s—was now distributing brochures. His demeanour was almost dismissive, and his bias was evident. He mispronounced almost every international name without blinking. It had become so routine, some had even Americanized their names. Murthi was now Monty; Tirupati had become Timothy; Velliar was called Wells.

When the instructor mispronounced Ankit's name while handing him the brochure, the latter decided to do something about it.

'Hey, it's a pretty simple name. Let me teach you the pronunciation—just so you do not embarrass yourself like this again.'

Identity Crisis

The room went quiet.

'Seriously?' the instructor glared.

'I'm every bit serious, Dr Billy.' Ankit said, reading the name off the staff badge around the instructor's neck. 'It's Ankit. *Ank-it*. Repeat after me: Ank-it.'

'Aan-khit?'

'No. Ank-it.'

It took nearly 15 tries before the instructor came anywhere close. Ankit's colleagues watched in bewilderment, some stifling grins, others unsure what to make of it. Just as Billy's discomfort was reaching a peak, Murthi spoke up quietly.

'It's *Moor-thee*, by the way. "Thee" as in thesis.' His voice was calm, almost gentle. Clear. He wasn't trying to make a scene—he just wanted to be heard.

The rest of the class watched silently as Billy's face flushed deeper, embarrassment and annoyance flitting across his features.

'Right, right. Moor-Thee. Got it.' Billy mumbled, eyes darting across the room, like he wished he could melt into the carpet.

Murthi sat back down, serene and unaffected, unaware of how deeply the moment had shifted the energy in the room.

⚭

The next two hours passed agonizingly slowly as a heated debate on ethics and professionalism unfolded. For the first time in his life, Ankit realized he was bad at something.

He'd had a full week to prepare for this seminar—he'd read the assigned material, even skimmed a few extra papers. But somehow, the depth and gravity of the subject had eluded him. It hit him, hard, how much he had underestimated it. The magnitude of his ignorance now stared him down, not just as a professional blind spot but as a personal failing.

And it wasn't just him. His whole team was struggling.

As the session went on, Ankit began to re-evaluate his earlier assumption. Billy's behaviour, which he had interpreted as bias, started to make more sense. It was not prejudice—it was annoyance, frustration. Frustration that, in hindsight, was justified.

Ankit felt a sinking realization settle in. This wasn't India. This wasn't the system he had trained in or grown used to. Here in the United States, doctors were much more than just individuals with medical education—they were communicators, counsellors, navigators through life-and-death decisions. The doctor–patient relationship here had layers he had never even thought to peel back.

The tension in the conference room felt almost stifling. Ankit found himself grappling with the weight of his own uncertainty. These weren't concepts that lived in textbooks—they were real, messy, and nuanced. *How do you treat a patient when there's no clear path? When every option has a cost? When reason fails and only perspective remains?*

Then Billy presented a case example that was strikingly insightful. Unexpectedly, his voice became the glue that held the fractured classroom together. He did not just present cases—he humanized them. He drew threads from moral philosophy, patient psychology, social context—layer upon layer—until Ankit was no longer sure whether he was learning ethics or something far more intimate about being human.

Ankit listened, quietly humbled. Perhaps he had overreacted earlier. Maybe his own defensiveness had clouded his judgement. He leaned into the conversation, this time with sincerity, asking sharper, thoughtful questions.

Billy noticed; his tone warmed. He acknowledged Ankit's insights. The room, once rigid with unease, now felt alive. The energy had shifted. Disagreement no longer felt like confrontation—it felt like growth. And for Ankit, it was more than just a good class; it was a moment of transformation. A revelation.

Even when people didn't agree—even when they came from vastly different training systems and worldviews—they could still listen. They could still keep the conversation going. That openness, he realized, was not just good academic practice—it was the cornerstone of meaningful relationships. Shutting down was not strength. Staying open was. As the seminar broke for the lunch, Ankit approached Billy.

'Hey,' he said, hesitating for a second before continuing. 'I just wanted to say—I'm sorry for earlier. I misread your behaviour. I thought it was biased, even discriminatory, but I get it now. You were annoyed… And you had every right to be. You probably saw this coming.'

Billy looked at him, not unkindly. 'It's okay. And

yeah... I do have this stereotype about Indian doctors when it comes to ethics. And I know how wrong it sounds—but I have been organizing these conferences for 15 years, and honestly, I'm still waiting to meet one who breaks the pattern.'

He paused, then added. 'It's not that they are bad or unprofessional—they're brilliant! But most have no idea how to interact with a patient or how to break bad news to the patient's family.'

Ankit nodded, this time without defensiveness. 'I agree with you. And you're right—there's context to that. In India, the healthcare system operates on a very different model. Everything revolves around volume—patients seen per day. Doctors are overvalued in theory but undervalued in practice. No one wants to pay for care, and to stay financially viable, we end up cutting corners. One-shot diagnoses, rushed consults, stacks of medications. Follow-ups are rare because they cost. Writing lab tests? That instantly triggers mistrust—patients think we're either incompetent or corrupt.'

Billy listened, his expression softening.

'And since pharmacies are unregulated,' Ankit continued, 'patients often self-medicate based on whatever the pharmacist recommends. We are the world's largest supplier of generics for a reason. And don't even get me started on quacks. From homoeopathy to Ayurvedic clinics and "herbal cures", people go anywhere before they go to an actual doctor. And then, when it's almost too late, when it's a life-threatening situation, they finally come to us.'

'I know, man. Sadly, that's true for most of South Asia,' Billy sighed.

Ankit nodded. He took a deep breath and said, I just want to say, thank you for being so open and for engaging today. I've always been a strong proponent of evidence-based medicine, but today reminded me how important ethics is—maybe more than I gave it credit for.'

Billy smiled. 'It's never too late to improve. If you are serious about it, there's a short online course our council provides. Worth looking into.' He pulled a card from his coat pocket. 'Here—take this.'

Ankit accepted the card, his fingers curling around its edge. For a moment, his mind flashed back to a scene from years ago—a senior surgeon had refused to operate on a critical patient because the family hadn't managed the advance deposit in time. He wondered what Billy would say if he shared that.

Billy's expression softened, as though some invisible weight had lifted, or at least eased. He hesitated, then spoke, his voice steady, tinged with something personal.

'I just want to say thank you,' he said, looking Ankit in the eye. 'Thank you for being open today. These conversations aren't easy—especially when there is so much to unpack—but you did it with grace, and I really respect that. I want to share something with you... something I do not talk about often, but I think it might help you understand where I am coming from.'

Ankit gave a slight nod, sensing the gravity behind the words.

'I have always believed in clinical science, like you. But my passion? It is not just academic. It comes from something deeply personal. Back in the 1980s, there was this device in the United States called the EPFX. It claimed to balance bioenergetic forces, promised all kinds of miraculous cures. It was nonsense—dangerous pseudoscience—but people believed in it. Many died because they did not seek proper medical help. It took 10 years for the device to be banned, but by then, the damage had already been done. More than 10,000 of those devices had been sold, and my family was among the victims. I lost people I loved because of it.'

Billy paused, his words hanging heavy in the air. 'That is what drove me here, to where I am today. That's why I do what I do. Why I challenge pseudoscience wherever I see it. But here's the thing—science alone doesn't always guide us. What's right or wrong… what's just or unjust… those aren't just scientific questions. They're ethical ones. And they're embedded in culture, in people's lived experiences. That's why I study ethics as seriously as I study evidence, even though I'm still learning how to balance the two.'

He shifted slightly, the intensity in his tone giving way to something softer.

'I know I can be blunt. I've been told that more times than I can count. I know my style can come off as abrasive. But today? I learnt a lot too. Your openness, your willingness to engage—even when we disagreed—that's what this work is really about.'

He smiled—genuine, appreciative.

'Ethics isn't just about finding the perfect answer. It's about navigating differences. About learning to sit with complexity. And about figuring out, together, how to move forward. One conversation at a time.'

∞

15

Caring for Oligarchs

Cafeteria, Oncology Department
Northbridge General Hospital

Ankit had been looking forward to a quiet break when a voice interrupted his thoughts.

'Dr Ankit, I've been looking for you. Your phone was unreachable.'

Sighing, he set his sandwich down and turned. A tall, broad-shouldered African-American man stood in front of him—Jackson, the medical technician.

Ankit had always believed—backed by data and cold economic truth—that if you were born poor, the odds of rising above it were slim. Yet, in his career, it was often people like them who left the biggest mark. The unsung heroes. Those who didn't make headlines or publish papers but held the system together through sheer dedication. Jackson was one of those people.

He had grown up in a tough neighbourhood, raised by a single mother. Life had offered him every excuse to grow bitter or spiral down, but Jackson had chosen another path—resilience. During Ankit's induction, Jackson had shared his story. His struggles. The sacrifices his mother had made. The many obstacles he had overcome. It had been a deeply moving conversation and had left a lasting impression on Ankit.

Jackson had also been one of the first to welcome him. His handshake had been warm and sincere, accompanied by a simple yet reassuring, 'Welcome, Doc, I'm here to help you.' The gesture had brought a comfort Ankit hadn't anticipated.

Over time, Jackson proved to be exactly that—reliable, supportive, always ready to help. During high-pressure and chaotic moments, especially with Dr Silva's rapid-fire instructions, Jackson would step in with calm clarity: 'This is what she probably meant.' In those moments, when the room felt like it was spinning, Jackson restored order.

Although Jackson didn't have a wall full of prestigious degrees or accolades, Ankit knew—beyond a shadow of a doubt—that he was indispensable. Where others came and went, Jackson stayed. A constant. A steadying presence who held the team together. He eased tensions with jokes, brought levity on tough days and created a sense of camaraderie that made even the hardest shifts bearable. On game days, he proudly wore his football jersey, cheering for his team, his laughter echoing through the halls and lifting everyone's spirits.

Jackson reminded Ankit a lot of Johnny; both men carried the weight of difficult pasts, and both embodied a kind of quiet strength that Ankit had come to admire deeply. Back home, it was Johnny who had taught Ankit the unspoken rules of working in a high-pressure hospital and had guided him through more critical cases than he could count. Both men, continents apart, were cut from the same cloth.

To Ankit, Jackson was a true hero. His humility, his resilience, his way of showing up—not for glory but because it mattered. That was the kind of heroism no textbook could ever teach.

'Hey, Jackson! My shift just ended. What's up?'

'Dr Silva handed out fresh instructions. She wants you to attend to a new patient who just arrived. We'll get more details from admin.'

'All right, let's go,' Ankit said, rising from his chair. 'But why me? Aren't new patients usually assigned to junior doctors?'

Jackson gave a small nod and said, 'Yes, normally. But I think this might be an HPISU.'

'What's an HPISU? I've heard that term before.'

Jackson gave him a knowing look as they started walking towards the ward. 'You've probably noticed that sometimes we get international clients who don't have American health insurance. They bear the full cost. Insurance companies often negotiate deep discounts and delay payments. Then there are pro bono cases, non-profit referrals... All of that drains revenue. But HPISUs—High Profile International Service Users—they pay upfront. In full.'

Ankit frowned. 'So...you are saying they jump the queue? That having deep pockets gets them better treatment?'

Jackson thought for a moment before responding. 'I wouldn't say "better" exactly, but...it's not untrue. Having money opens doors. They skip the waiting. They don't go through referrals. They don't need pre-approvals or trial protocols. They just get in. It's not a question of fairness—it's just how the system works.'

He paused mid-stride. 'To be honest, I don't fully understand how it all works, but I've seen high-profile international clients come here for treatment. They pay higher rates. And while I'd argue that the quality of care here is excellent for everyone, it's undeniable that those with money have options that others don't. They can extend their stays, access experimental trials or participate in ongoing research programmes. That kind of flexibility comes with the ability to pay out of pocket.'

Ankit nodded as he absorbed the information.

'Healthcare in this country is expensive,' Jackson added, his tone turning more serious. 'Without insurance or government support, it's practically a recipe for bankruptcy—unless you're a billionaire. That's the reality. Hospitals like Northbridge, a top-tier oncology centre, thrive because they're tertiary institutes. People come here when they've exhausted all other options. They'll pay anything just to buy a little more time. It's heartbreaking, really. That's why places like this flourish while smaller hospitals in rural communities barely stay afloat. They just don't have the same resources and rely heavily on government aid.'

Ankit listened intently, slowly realizing how deep the disparities ran. The healthcare system didn't just favour the rich—it was built for them.

'It's not perfect,' Jackson said with a quiet sigh, 'but

it's the reality we work with. The system has its flaws, and yeah, it's frustrating. But the team here does everything they can to provide the best care possible—regardless of the patient's financial background.'

'It's complicated, for sure. But I guess it's important to understand how it all works... Even if it's a hard pill to swallow.'

Jackson gave him a slight smile. 'Complicated is an understatement, Doc. But it's the world we live in, and we just do our best to make a difference where we can.'

As they reached the admin desk and asked for the patient files, Ankit found himself lost in thought. The quiet injustice of the system gnawed at him. Still, he appreciated Jackson's honesty.

'Why do we even need insurance companies?' he asked suddenly. 'Why can't there be a single-payer system like in other countries? Why isn't healthcare affordable for everyone?'

Jackson's face softened. 'You know, back in 1973, there was a healthcare bill passed to regulate care. But it wasn't until 1980 that insurance companies began managing it, with the idea of making healthcare more accessible and equitable. But, like most good ideas, it got corrupted. Managed-care companies started using algorithms to decide who gets care and who doesn't. Administrators pocket the profits, and some of the least qualified people are making decisions that should be left to doctors. If you ask anyone who's had to deal with the system here, they'll have a story to tell. It's a mess... But no one knows how to fix it.'

Just then, the admin returned with a file in hand. 'High-profile client. Referred by the Ambassador himself. We need to take special care of them,' he said, pointing towards the waiting room.

Jackson glanced at the file and muttered, 'Told you—HPISU. Seventy-one, second-stage cancer; came with the whole family.'

'Wow, Jackson. You really know how this collection department works,' Ankit replied as they started walking towards the waiting room.

'Oh yeah,' Jackson said with a half-smile. 'Had a run-in with them last year. My uncle needed an MRI, and they charged him $5,000. Then the collection department kept harassing him, calling daily. I knew a few people here, so we used the beneficiary fund to settle it for much less.'

Ankit raised an eyebrow. 'I thought the beneficiary fund was for low-income families.'

Jackson nodded, but his expression darkened. 'It's supposed to be. But the truth is, it's more about maintaining non-profit status for tax breaks. The money doesn't always go where it should. It's a system meant to help...but it doesn't always work that way.'

Ankit was taken aback. 'The system here isn't as fair as I thought,' he rued.

Jackson gave a soft, tired laugh. 'Doc, you'd be shocked if you knew the half of it. The healthcare system is more like an industry. It's not built to be fair—it's built to function. And it functions in ways that people like us will never fully understand.'

Ankit felt his frustration simmering as he and Jackson entered the room. They found an elderly woman sitting there with her family.

'I'm Dr Ankit,' he introduced himself.

The family eyed him with disappointment as a man, who appeared to be the patient's son, said, 'Where is Dr Silva? We came here for her.'

'Dr Silva will see you tomorrow. I'm here to understand your medical history,' Ankit informed them.

'Oh, he's just the errand boy,' the man muttered dismissively.

Ankit stood there for a beat, then quietly excused himself, the sting of humiliation washing over him. He found Jackson just outside the room. 'They looked straight through me,' Ankit said, shaking his head. 'Why didn't I speak up?'

Jackson studied him for a moment, then said, 'Sounds like a bully. Why didn't you tell them your designation?'

Ankit exhaled. 'It reminded me of how I grew up. That instinct to stay silent around power, authority—to avoid confrontation. Especially with people who might retaliate. I froze. I should've stood up for myself. But I didn't want to seem entitled or difficult. I've carried that mindset for years, and in that moment, it just came back. I've been in situations like this before, and I've always felt powerless.'

Jackson nodded. 'It's like not eating in your own restaurant…and ordering food from someone else's.'

Ankit couldn't help but laugh, the tension easing slightly, as he went back to the waiting room.

16

Education without Wisdom

Ankit's House

'You did what?' Pooja shrieked with laughter as Ankit recounted the story.

'I replaced the sugar sachets with salt.'

'God damn, Ankit, you're hilarious.'

'Hey, I was pissed. Can you blame me? They were so disappointed to see me—visibly let down. They clearly believe white doctors are better than people like us. The entire hour I spent with them, they kept shooting not-so-subtle glances at me. It felt awful. I had to do something. It's like when brown folks demand a white pilot and refuse to fly with someone from their own country. It's a psychological twister.'

'I know the daughter-in-law—her name is Jyoti. We were classmates. Her family is one of those landlord types. She comes from old money. Her great-grandfather was awarded the title of "Rai Bahadur" by the British, and her grandfather was a union minister back in the day.'

'Were you guys friends?' Ankit asked.

'Not even close. She was one of "those" girls. Elite clique. Snobby. Barely acknowledged the rest of us. Then she somehow landed an Oxbridge scholarship and moved abroad. Which, honestly, was a sheer waste of resources if you ask me; she married some businessman soon after—who, by the way, is now a cabinet minister from the ruling party—and he doesn't even let her work. I spoke to her yesterday. Apparently, she has support staff and domestic help for everything, and all she does is order them around. Still, she whines on social media about how hard her life is and posts those cringey inspirational quotes about women's empowerment. People like her make me sick.'

'Yeah, I saw her bossing around that maid,' Ankit replied, his voice darkening. 'She can't be more than 18; I wonder how they were able to get a visa for her. Yesterday, I was pretty sure Jyoti was about to hit her over something ridiculously petty. She only stopped when she realized I was in the room.'

He exhaled, jaw clenched. 'When you are up close to people like that, it hits you how much injustice we've normalized in our society. How can one be *born* into a lower class or caste? Aren't we all born equal? Isn't that literally what reasoning is supposed to lead us to? But try bringing this up at home and you get hit with straw man arguments about tradition and culture. It makes me so angry—and honestly, ashamed. We talk about Eurocentric privilege like we're the victims, but we've built entire systems of discrimination back home. If we can't call out the bias and bigotry in our circles, then we're just hypocrites.'

'They probably lured her to the States with promises

of a good job and a better life,' Pooja commented in a quiet voice. 'And now she's stuck. Treated like a servant—maybe worse. She probably doesn't even know she deserves more.'

'I want to report it to the Department of Foreign Affairs,' Ankit said firmly. 'Get her out of here.'

'We can talk to Dr Jindal, or someone else at the hospital who might know how to handle this properly,' Pooja suggested. 'Either way, we'll meet them tomorrow. Dr Jindal is hosting a get-together at his place in the afternoon. Said your phone was unreachable, so he asked me to pass on the invite.'

17

Losing Chumships

Dr Jindal's House

'Dr Shashi, it's your turn now—what's the one memorably worst case you've ever seen?'

Ankit, Dr and Mrs Jindal, Dr Shashi, Pooja and Dr Goldstein were huddled around a small table on the patio at Dr Jindal's house, basking in the afternoon warmth, bellies full from Mrs Jindal's delightful culinary masterpieces.

Dr Shashi leaned back and sighed, his expression darkening with memory. 'This incident happened about 32 years ago,' he began. 'I was doing outpatient consultations at a government hospital—just a regular day. A couple came in carrying their daughter in their arms. She was around seven years old. By the way they dressed and behaved, it was obvious that they came from money—designer clothes, refined mannerisms. This alone was surprising because, in those days, only the poor or lower-middle class came to government hospitals.'

He paused, glancing at the group before continuing. 'Anyway, I asked what the issue was, and the parents showed me a large ulcer—about five by five centimetres—

on her left leg. The skin was totally denuded, and the muscles were exposed. Normally, such ulcers show up in the underprivileged—those who can't maintain proper hygiene. But this girl seemed to be from a wealthy family. They told me they had consulted many private doctors, but nothing had worked. That's why they had come to the government hospital as a last resort.'

Dr Shashi's voice grew quieter. 'My first instinct was to think about diabetes. But the parents denied it; diabetic ulcers are very rare at that age anyway. Could it be an immune disorder? HIV, maybe? Unlikely. Then I considered a neurological issue—maybe she didn't feel pain in that leg, which would explain the neglect of the wound. That seemed like a fair possibility. But why the loss of sensation?'

He looked around the table. 'Her sensorium was intact, so the brain was not the issue. I zeroed in on the spinal cord. I asked if she had ever experienced back trauma. What they said next stunned me—she had meningomyelocele, operated on unsuccessfully when she was an infant.'

Mrs Jindal leaned forward, frowning. 'What's that?'

'It is a neural tube defect,' Dr Shashi explained. 'The spinal cord and its protective coverings—the meninges—protrude outside the spinal canal. That kind of damage leads to paralysis and loss of sensation, often in the lower limbs. She couldn't control her bladder or bowels either.'

He paused. 'The ulcer made sense then. Constant pressure on her limb, no sensation, no feedback to move or adjust. Add to that the dribbling of urine onto the wound—it was in a terrible state. I checked her reports—she already had kidney damage from backflow. She was just seven; it was even scary to think about the future of that child.'

The group sat in silence for a moment.

'This is heartbreaking, Dr Shashi,' Pooja finally said. 'I don't think AI could ever reason through that the way you did. That's advanced human deductive thinking. Is there a cure for this?'

'Not as of yet, but prevention is key. Folic acid supplementation before and during pregnancy can help reduce the risks. In fact, it is one of the rare conditions where doctors recommend starting supplements even before conception, when a couple is planning for a child. The brain and spinal cord develop by the fourth week post-fertilization—many people don't even know they're pregnant by then.' He paused, then added, 'There are other causes too—genetics, medication side effects, environmental factors—it's not always about folic acid alone.'

'I read somewhere that early teenage pregnancies—like among 13- to 15-year-old girls—have a much higher incidence of meningomyelocele,' Dr Goldstein offered.

'Yes, Dr Goldstein, you're absolutely right,' Dr Shashi nodded. 'Oh, that reminds me! I saw a young Indian girl yesterday in the cafeteria. She was just standing there, watching people eat. She looked so lost. I tried to speak to her, but she ran off. Poor thing seemed terrified. Does anyone know who she is?'

'Ah yes, Dr Shashi, I think you're talking about the

girl staying with the old Indian lady who is admitted to our oncology department. She came with the family; think she is their house help. They treat her horribly. I'm sure they pulled some sketchy shit to get her a visa,' Ankit said, his voice tinged with concern. 'Can we do something to help her, Dr Jindal?'

Dr Jindal gave his long nose a thoughtful scratch, then said, 'I doubt we can do anything legally. They seem to have all the right documents—at least enough to get her through immigration. Even if we prove she is being mistreated, Child Protection Services would probably just hand her over to the embassy since she is not a US citizen. And with the kind of money this family has, you can bet they will meddle with the process. But... I have a friend who works in the embassy; let me talk to her and find out what options we have. Can you find out the girl's name and the date they arrived?'

'I know the patient's daughter-in-law,' Pooja chimed in. 'I'll try to get the details from her.'

'Do you think your friend in the embassy will be able to help, Dr Jindal?' asked Ankit.

'She should; she's the Head of Chancery there.'

'Wait—are you talking about Mrs Bhatnagar by any chance?' asked Dr Shashi. 'I know her as well!'

'You do? How?' Dr Jindal asked, his eyebrows raised.

'Well, it's an embarrassing—but kind of hilarious—story. I was in Germany a few years ago and got pulled over while driving. I didn't even realize I'd broken a rule. The officer asked for my papers, and like a complete idiot, I tried to bribe him. I actually held his arm to pull him aside and, with a €50 note in my pocket, moved towards him. You can imagine how that went. I got arrested immediately—and it made the news across the EU.'

'Oh, was that you?' Pooja exclaimed, wide-eyed. 'I was in the UK then—I remember watching it on the news: "Indian doctor arrested for assault and bribery". That's the stupidest thing you could have done in that situation.'

The group burst into laughter.

'Mrs Bhatnagar was with the embassy there at the time,' Dr Shashi went on, 'and she helped me out—arranged for a lawyer and even smoothed things over with the medical board.'

'What happened with the board?' Pooja asked.

'Well,' Dr Shashi sighed, 'I had to apply for a "fit to practise" licence there. When the charges were eventually dropped, my lawyer had to appear before the board and explain everything to the panel.'

Dr Shashi paused, his expression softening. 'It was…complicated,' he said slowly, his voice tinged with vulnerability. 'At that time, I had to undergo a psychological evaluation. I still remember the strange mix of relief and humiliation I felt when they told me I was a savant. It finally explained why I had always felt different—why I kept stumbling into situations that others seemed to navigate effortlessly.'

The group quietened, attention shifting. 'I was bullied a lot as a kid,' Dr Shashi continued. 'For the longest time, I thought maybe I was just unlucky… Or maybe I was broken in some way. I have always been good at solving puzzles and understanding abstract systems. But people? Reading people, understanding their motives... that was like trying to see through frosted glass. My brain just did not process their thoughts or intentions the way most people's brains do.'

He drew a breath. 'Eventually, they diagnosed me with a mild form of Asperger's. That label brought clarity, but also shame. I had picked up certain behaviours from one cultural context—things that were perfectly normal back home—but when I repeated them abroad, they were illegal. I didn't even realize what I was doing was wrong.'

Dr Shashi let out a dry, rueful laugh. 'To me, it felt like just another fine to pay—another small hurdle to cross. But during the evaluation, one of the panellists looked at my records and remarked, "You are clearly brilliant. Your scores are off the charts. Why would someone like you try to manipulate the system?" That is when they referred me for further testing.'

He looked up, meeting their eyes. 'The evaluation answered a lot of the questions that had plagued me over the years. I was not trying to cheat the system—I simply did not see it the way others did. Since then, I have worked hard to bridge that gap. I have had mentors and guides who have helped me understand situations my brain isn't wired to naturally grasp.'

There was a moment of stunned silence, the group visibly moved by the raw honesty of Dr Shashi's words.

'By the way, Dr Pooja,' Dr Jindal finally broke the silence. 'I had no idea you practised in the UK. How was it?'

'Oh, Arjun and I applied for a residency there just

after our wedding. We saw some advertisement somewhere and acted on impulse. It's a decision I regret and cherish at the same time.'

'I didn't get that,' Ankit said, puzzled.

'I regret the decision because the residency there was nothing like we imagined,' Pooja explained. 'There's a lot of prejudice, bias and bigotry you have to face. I remember every time we went to a restaurant, white folks got better service. Ironically, that even happened at Asian-owned joints. I could go on and on. Arjun was mistaken for a cab driver numerous times. He'd be driving to work, and people would wave him down, thinking he was a cabbie.'

'Ah yes, I can attest to that as well,' Dr Shashi agreed.

'Then why do you say you cherish the decision?' Ankit persisted.

'How do I put it into words?... You know how a difficult environment brings out your true self? All the hardships we faced there made me realize the kind of man I had actually married. I saw a side of Arjun I hadn't seen before—shallow, rigid. Things got bad between us fast, and it was there that I decided to divorce him. Soon after, I applied for a residency in the US and moved here.'

'Cheers to lessons in life and new beginnings,' Dr Jindal said, raising his glass.

Everyone joined in, and the conversation naturally meandered in a different direction, an easy camaraderie replacing the earlier tense atmosphere.

But Ankit's curiosity was not satisfied; he wanted to dig deeper and decided to wait until they were alone.

Later, as the evening settled into a comfortable stillness and everyone began heading home, Ankit saw his chance and seized it.

'I'm sorry about you and Arjun,' he said as they walked, 'but I have to admit…I'm a little relieved. That guy was a real jerk back in college.'

'A little?' Pooja teased, raising an eyebrow.

'Okay, maybe more than a little,' Ankit admitted, grinning.

Pooja chuckled, shaking her head. 'You're cute, Ankit. And yeah, even I don't know what I saw in him. I have this habit of dating the wrong kinds of guys. I always thought I could find something deeper in him, but… trust me—if it's not obvious, don't wait around. What's not there probably isn't going to appear.'

'Did you date anyone else after him?' Ankit asked.

'Yeah. When I started my residency here, I met Phil— he was from Texas. As I found out later, he was an even bigger jerk. We were engaged. I almost married him. But when things started getting difficult, he just backed off and said it wasn't working any more. At least Arjun didn't give up that fast.'

Ankit, though a little hesitant, couldn't help but ask, 'Does that mean your preferences have shifted back to the subcontinent?'

Pooja gave him a sly smile. 'Depends,' she replied playfully.

A warm flush crept over Ankit's face. He reached up instinctively to play with his—his go-to move whenever he felt overwhelmed. His awkward body language betrayed his inner storm: a strange mix of elation and unease. There was joy—because her flirtation felt genuine. There was desire—to be seen, to be wanted. But there was also fear. Was this real or just playful banter? Was there a signal buried in the noise?

'Stop blushing, you idiot. I'm just messing around with you,' Pooja laughed.

Ankit smiled, heart pounding, unsure if the ground beneath his feet was shifting—or if he was just imagining it.

∞

18

Can't Remember but Can't Forget

Dr Silva's Office
Northbridge General Hospital

Vultures circled in, gradually.

On a bright, sunny day in June 1987, an unusually frail woman lay outdoors on a cot, burning with fever. She was waiting to die. Her young daughter sat beside her, gently pressing wet strips of cloth to her forehead.

'I wanted to make besan laddu for you one last time. I know how much you love them,' the woman whispered.

'Maa, what are you saying? Make as many laddus as you want,' the little girl said with innocent conviction, too young to grasp the finality of her mother's words.

'You see those vultures?' the woman asked, her voice raspy. 'Even they know I have only a few hours left. I can feel it in my bones.'

Overhead, the vultures shrieked—eerily, as if in agreement.

'Dr Silva?'

The voice pulled Dr Silva out of her reverie. The vultures and their shrieks faded as she blinked, jolting back into the present. Rachel stood in front of her, concern written across her face.

'You're as white as a sheet, and you're sweating,' Rachel said, handing Dr Silva a box of tissues. 'Are you okay?'

'I'm fine. What is it?'

'Shukla called. He said he's located the origin of the art form—and the makers of the bangles. It's a remote area in east-central India. He also mentioned that he has more information he's willing to *trade*, when you're ready.'

'Good,' Dr Silva said. 'I want to go there myself—sometime next month. Please clear my calendar for at least a week.'

'Sure. May I ask you something, Doctor?'

'Go ahead,' Silva replied, already bracing herself.

'Why is this information so important? Shukla said we were lucky—another high-profile family from the area, who'd come to him for help arranging medical treatment abroad, happened to recognize the bangles in those pictures. He promised them the best care. They're apparently in urgent need of funds—for treatment.'

'The story is long,' Silva said quietly, 'and not one I wish to revisit right now. Maybe some other time. Anything else?'

She drifted back into thought. How could she explain why she'd asked Shukla to find that information, when even she wasn't sure what she would do with it?

Ever since receiving those bangles as a gift, she'd felt a deep, inexplicable yearning—to reconcile with a broken past, to answer the fragmented, haunting dreams that had slowly begun to form into discernible shapes. The art on the bangles was native to the region where she'd been born. She could vaguely recall her mother wearing similar ones. The sight of them awakened a longing—to return to the land of her early memories, a place that had always felt like a phantom limb.

That's very unusual of Dr Silva. I wonder why she's so adamant about going there, Rachel thought. 'Oh—Dr Hawker wants to see you immediately. Dr Goldstein as well,' she informed her boss.

'What for?'

'I don't know for sure, but I think it's about that patient you declined to see... The elderly Indian lady. She's been reassigned to Dr Goldstein. I think he wants to review the treatment regimen with you.'

'And the Director?'

'Likely the same reason. He wasn't pleased when he heard you refused the case.'

'Call him.'

Rachel blinked. 'Uh, ma'am... He asked to see you *in person*, in his cabin.'

'And I'm asking you to call him,' Silva said, her tone calm but firm—still haunted by the image of circling vultures.

'Right away.'

Earlier that morning, Dr Silva had walked into Dr Goldstein's office without knocking, a thick binder tucked under her arm. 'This one's yours,' she said simply, placing it on his desk.

He looked up. 'The patient from India? You're handing it off?'

Dr Silva nodded. 'Yes.'

Goldstein studied her face, but didn't press. He'd worked with her long enough to know when not to ask questions. 'Understood,' he said, sliding the file towards himself.

Dr Silva had given a small nod and left without another word.

A few minutes later, Rachel's voice came through again, informing Dr Silva that the Director was on the line.

Dr Silva took a breath. 'Director? You wanted to see me?'

'Uh, yes. Can you come to my cabin, please?'

'No. We can talk here—on the phone.'

'It's about the patient you declined to see. May I ask why?'

'No.'

If she started to explain, that's all she would be doing for the rest of the day.

The Director, who had known Dr Silva for 22 years, was still caught off guard by her bluntness 'But, Doctor, they came all the way from India—for the best treatment.'

'And I can assure you, sir, that Dr Goldstein is perfectly capable of providing it. I do not wish to disclose the reason I declined her case. And this conversation is over.'

Dr Silva was perhaps the only person in the building who could talk to the Director like that—and hang up on him—and not face consequences.

She sank back into her chair, and once again, the vultures returned.

So did the image of the daughter and the dying mother...and the old woman in the oncology department. There had been something painfully familiar about the elderly woman's face—something that tugged at the edges of memory. But Silva couldn't quite place it.

She began speaking aloud, trying to navigate the confusion swirling within her.

'Am I angry? Am I a bad person? Am I even human? Am I alive?'

A pause.

'Am I so weak that my emotions are dictating my decisions? Who should I listen to?'

Tears welled in her eyes.

It's intractable. Invisible pain with no symptoms. *What is this? Why should I help her—and why not?*

There was a sharp contrast between Dr Silva's outward persona and her inner world. To the world, she was articulate, meticulous, soft-spoken—an embodiment of grace under pressure. Her professionalism and consistency made her a role model among colleagues.

But small quirks sometimes betrayed her inner fragility.

She struggled to reconcile her vulnerability with the polished façade she had built over the years. That emotional split often manifested as ambivalence—sometimes even harshness in the face of personal dilemmas. Though she sometimes caught herself in these spirals and reflected on them, self-awareness alone wasn't enough to keep them from happening.

There were moments when she deeply wished for someone to talk to—someone she could trust with the truth of her inner life. But where could she go? Who could she trust? She'd never allowed herself to be fully seen, and that refusal had created a private cage of silence.

Many wondered if her occasional outbursts were subconscious cries for help—or simply signs of the heavy emotional burden she bore quietly.

With the weight of indecision still pressing against her chest, Dr Silva made a decision.

Tonight, I'll get a drink.

19

Privilege

Cafeteria, Oncology Department
Northbridge General Hospital

'*Cogito ergo sum*,' Ankit blurted out of nowhere.

'Is that a new pasta dish?' Pooja asked, a teasing smile on her lips.

'No, it's a quote by Descartes. It means "I think, therefore I am,"' Ankit chuckled.

'I swear, Ankit, you're slowly turning into Dr Jindal with all your trivia and random facts.'

They were having lunch together—something of a daily ritual by now.

'Don't be mean,' Ankit retorted, pouting playfully. 'I was just trying to impress you with something I read recently. Speaking of which, Dr Jindal was asking about you yesterday. Were you able to find out about that young girl?'

'Oh yes—her name is Maya. I haven't been able to find out their day of arrival, though, but I am sure it must be in the hospital records. Do you have access to their files?'

'No... I'll ask Dr Silva.'

'You can ask her right now,' Pooja said, nodding towards the entrance. Dr Silva had just walked in.

'Dr Silva, do you have a moment?' Ankit approached her.

'Yes, Ankit?'

'I was wondering if I could access the files of Mrs Jaya Bhargava—the patient in Room 206. I just wanted to review the regimen again.'

'You can have access,' Dr Silva replied coolly. 'But only if you tell me honestly why you want it.'

'Uh, Doctor... As I said... I wanted to go over—'

'—the regimen again?' Silva cut in smoothly. 'If you had actually gone through it the first time, you'd know I am not the one handling her case, Dr Ankit; Dr Goldstein is. So, what is this really about?'

'Um... Actually, we are trying to confirm her day of arrival at the hospital,' Pooja interjected.

'And who are you?' Dr Silva asked, turning to her.

'Oh, this is Dr Pooja—from Emergency,' Ankit said. 'Doctor, the patient has a maid—a young girl—and the whole family treat her horribly. We suspect they did something sketchy to get a visa for her. We've already spoken to Dr Jindal; he has some contacts in the embassy. All we need is the girl's name and day of arrival. We have got the name—it's Maya.'

A subtle but immediate shift passed over Dr Silva's face. Sadness flickered in her eyes—then was quickly replaced by something colder. Contempt. Anger.

'That's appalling,' Dr Silva said, her voice rising. 'Some people never learn. And I thought slavery had been abolished. This is systemic oppression—of a young girl, a fellow human being. And it will never stop if we don't speak up.'

It was the most Ankit or Pooja had ever heard her say outside of a medical discussion. 'Thank you for your stance,' Ankit said quietly.

'Well, only tables and dead people don't take a stance,' she remarked. 'Human rights violations happen when good people turn a blind eye—because it doesn't affect them.'

Then, without another word, Dr Silva turned and started walking towards the exit.

'Come with me,' she called out. 'I have their file in my office.'

20

Hate Nobody

Office of the Dean
Northbridge General Hospital

Dean Hawker sighed in frustration as the overweight Indian man—decked out in every visible luxury brand—barrelled into his office. 'We came all the way here for Dr Silva. It's been three days, and she hasn't visited even once,' the man bellowed. 'Instead, we have been handed off to some Indian junior doctor and a Black ward boy. And now some Dr Goldy and another Indian doctor are handling my mother's case?'

'Dr Goldstein,' the dean corrected calmly. 'His name is Goldstein. And the other one is Dr Shashi. They are all here.' Hawker pointed towards the two men near the window, accompanied by Ankit, who was standing a little farther off. 'I assure you, sir, they are among our finest doctors. I apologize for the inconvenience; Dr Silva fell ill unexpectedly,' he finished.

'Nonsense. I saw her this afternoon. I know it was her. She visited every room in the wing except ours. Tell me the truth—if it's money, I can pay more.'

'Mr Bhargava,' Hawker began in a firm tone, 'I can

assure you this isn't about money. Dr Silva has too many patients, and due to health concerns, she is not taking any new ones. Dr Goldstein was her personal recommendation. And Dr Shashi is one of the best surgeons in the country. He will be performing the resection.'

Sanjay Bhargava turned to Dr Shashi. 'Are you really as good as the dean claims?'

'I like to think I am better,' Dr Shashi replied flippantly. 'I can share my data with you—it's just a few pages long. I'm not sure if you'll understand, though—the last time I showed it to someone, they were clueless. Maybe you'd prefer the star ratings from an independent board? I have been awarded seven stars.'

'I know how those ratings work,' Sanjay smirked. 'Anyone can get those.'

Dr Shashi didn't even flinch. 'Go ahead. Try getting one with *that* board and let me know how long it takes. We can meet after; I need to go now.'

Sanjay opened his mouth, but Dr Shashi didn't stop.

'People like you—rude, entitled, utterly unfit for public service, are exactly why our education system is in ruins and the talent pool is bleeding out. You are the reason thousands like me leave everything behind—family, friends, home—and work in another country just to be recognized. So, thanks, but no thanks. You can take your money and shove it. And let me do my job. If you have any reservations about my skills, you're free to take your mother elsewhere.'

There was a stunned silence. Then Dr Shashi pressed on. 'When I applied for a surgical registrar post back home, I was the top candidate. The role went to Sanya, who was my classmate. Her only merit? A politically connected marriage. She barely showed up—only came to collect her salary and benefits, and no one dared question her.

'Need more examples, Mr Bhargava?'

Sanjay stood frozen, like a deer in headlights. No one had ever spoken to him like this before. As the shock wore off, it curdled into rage.

'Do you have any idea who you're talking to, you bastard?' Sanjay seethed.

'Do *you* have any idea where you are standing?' Dr Shashi replied coolly. 'This isn't India. Here, the law protects me. And the same law might find you guilty of child abuse—if someone reported how you treat that young girl.'

Ankit's eyes widened as he watched the showdown, speechless.

'I know what you'd do if this were India,' Dr Shashi continued his charge. 'Either force people to collude or punish them for defiance. A close friend of mine who went back home to practise was fired after politely asking the hospital construction team to reduce noise near a neurologically unstable patient. The constructor said, "You foreign-return doctors don't know how to behave; this is India." So no, Mr Bhargava, you don't scare me. I suggest you sit down quietly, stop undermining my expertise and let me work.'

Dr Hawker, having watched in tense silence, finally intervened. 'Whoa—hang on a minute. This is getting out of hand,' he said sharply. 'Dr Shashi, I think you need a moment to reflect on your words. I understand this is a heated discussion, but this is a *hospital*; this is not how we conduct ourselves.'

He then turned to Sanjay. 'You are here for your mother's care. I expect you to treat our staff with respect. We all must maintain a level of decorum—this is not the place for personal attacks.'

He then turned back to Dr Shashi. 'Doctor, please meet me in my office. We need to talk.'

As the dean exited, Dr Shashi started following him out.

Ankit caught up to him. 'This is the gutsiest thing I've ever seen... Aren't you scared?' he asked, his voice low. 'Back home, the head of the cardiac department at my old hospital had to touch a politician's feet for making him wait half an hour. I can't imagine the consequences of what you just did.'

'It's high time someone gave these assholes a reality check,' Dr Shashi muttered under his breath. Then he paused, looked at Ankit, and took a breath. 'But... I think I crossed a line.'

Ankit blinked, clearly shaken.

'I shouldn't have said all that,' Dr Shashi continued. 'The dean is clearly unhappy with me, and I am probably in for another warning. If I keep this up, I could face disciplinary action. I'm at a different stage in my career, Ankit—and I would strongly advise you not to follow in my footsteps.

'I know I have a problem—I mentioned it the

other day at Dr Jindal's house. Still, I should not let my frustration get the better of me. But this isn't just a personal issue—it's a systemic rot. And we need a proper review mechanism to address it, not emotional outbursts like mine.' He paused again, then added with quiet sincerity, 'I know what Dr Hawker is going to say. And honestly? He'll be right. I want to apologize—to you. I haven't been the best role model. These are my limitations, my flaws, and I am aware of them. I hope you can understand and accept that. This is certainly not the kind of behaviour I want you to emulate.'

With that, he walked off, leaving Ankit standing in silence—staring after him with something close to awe.

21

Transcending Bystander Effect

Oncology Department
Northbridge General Hospital

Dr Silva's day, as always, began with a strong double shot of hazelnut espresso and a brisk morning bulletin from Rachel.

'Dr Jindal from Anaesthesia called. He said to let you know the embassy cannot do much. All the documents checked out, and the family has political backing. The ruling party's, to be precise. He says we'll need to find another—'

Before Rachel could finish her sentence, Dr Silva was already on her feet and out the door.

Her heels echoed as she moved swiftly down the long hallway—past the cafeteria, past the nurses' station—her white coat billowing behind her like a banner. The hospital corridors were beginning to stir with the day's first rhythms. In the general ward, half the patients were still snoring; others blinked sleep from their eyes and watched curiously as she breezed by.

Then came the private wing.
201…
202…
204…
And then—206.

Outside the room, on a hard, narrow wooden bench, a young girl was curled up asleep. No blanket. No pillow. Her body looked small, frail, almost folded in on itself, like a question mark no one had answered.

Dr Silva paused. For a moment, she just stood there, watching the way sunlight filtered through the window and caught the girl's hair—turning it into threads of gold. Her face was the most beautiful Dr Silva had seen in a long, long time. A tightness crept into her chest.

Gently, she reached out and placed her hand on the girl's head. The girl woke with a start and her gaze met Dr Silva's—wide-eyed, confused, vulnerable.

No words were exchanged.

Dr Silva brushed a thumb along her cheek. The girl didn't flinch.

Then, with a slight nod and a soft tug of her fingers, Dr Silva beckoned her.

And just like that, the girl stood. Sleep still in her bones, eyes heavy, but something deep within her trusted this stranger. Without hesitation, she slipped her hand into Dr Silva's. They walked away together, hand in hand.

No explanation. No questions. Just a moment of intuitive understanding.

How strange! Sometimes, we act without thinking. Sometimes, we understand without words.

22

Indoctrination: The Pathway to a Curated Life

Cafeteria, Oncology Department
Northbridge General Hospital

'I'm exhausted. I need sleep, not breakfast,' Ankit whined as Pooja dragged him towards a table.

Their 12-hour night shifts had just ended, and Pooja was determined to grab a quick bite before heading home. A few days ago, Ankit had asked her to move in.

Pooja and Ankit had become inseparable over the last few weeks—much to Dr Jindal's delight. He kept reminding them—with exaggerated pride—that it was at *his* party and *his* house where they had met again and rekindled their old flame. So much so that Dr Shashi had nicknamed him 'Cupid'.

Pulling both of Ankit's cheeks, Pooja tried to cheer him up. 'You look such a cutie when you are grumpy,' she giggled.

But Ankit's attention was elsewhere. He had suddenly gone quiet and was looking past Pooja. Not getting a response, she turned to follow his gaze.

Dr Silva was coming from the ward area—and walking beside her was Maya, the young girl.

Startled, both of them stood up to intercept her.

'Dr Silva!'

'The embassy lead we were pursuing... It did not work out,' she informed them. 'I don't know what we will do next... Their documents checked out and the family has political clout. They're with the ruling party. But I know this much—I cannot let her be with that family one more minute.'

Tears welled in her eyes as she stormed off. Maya followed at her heel, while Ankit and Pooja trailed behind.

'Are you taking her to your office, Doctor?' Pooja asked gently.

'No. I'm taking her to my house. She'll stay there until we figure out what to do.'

'We can come with you, Doctor. Lend a hand. Our shifts are over anyway,' Ankit offered.

'Aren't you two tired? I'm going to drop her off, settle her in and come back to work.'

'No, no, we're okay. We'll keep her company till you return,' Ankit insisted.

∽∞∾

Ankit could feel a strange emotional heaviness in the air as the four of them sped through the morning traffic in Dr Silva's Maserati. Maya still hadn't spoken a word. Then it struck him—they had been conversing in English. That poor child probably had not understood a single word.

Indoctrination: The Pathway to a Curated Life

And yet, there she sat, her face calm and trusting. She knew, somehow, that she was safe now and among good, kind people. *That,* Ankit mused, *is the power of empathy and non-verbal language.*

From the driver's seat, Dr Silva occasionally glanced at Maya through the rear-view mirror. Ankit had never seen the doctor like this before—so vulnerable. To him, Dr Silva had always been an emblem of dignified composure, precision and clinical detachment.

Pooja, meanwhile, was wrestling with her own thoughts.

'These people… They're so arrogant,' she muttered, louder than intended.

'Arrogance,' Dr Silva replied quietly, 'is a great obstruction to wisdom. And anger shuts down parts of your brain that govern judgement. It gives all your power to someone else.'

Pooja froze; she had heard these exact words before.

A different country, a different car, but she had been sitting in the same position—by the window seat, traffic rushing past. Memories flooded her. She had just landed in the UK with Arjun and they were headed to the hospital-provided accommodation. Pooja had been looking out the window as Arjun sat beside her in the cab, flipping through his exam prep book, frustration brewing.

Suddenly, he slammed the book shut. 'I don't get why we have to keep proving ourselves again and again,' he fumed. 'Why isn't the international licence good enough for these twats here?'

'Because, sadly, people back home are bigger twats. No quality control. Corruption. Zero transparency in the examination process. Need I remind you how you got *your* licence, Arjun?'

'I would have passed the exam easily if I'd tried. It was just stupid to waste time on it. Papa had connections in the board—so I did the smart thing. But yeah, I would have easily passed.'

'I'm sure you could have.'

'Are you guys from Asia?' their cab driver asked.

Pooja looked at him closely and realized he also looked Asian.

'Yes, we're. Are you Indian?'

'I'm Kashmiri,' the driver replied.

'Yeah, that's India,' Arjun stated.

'No, sir; I belong to Azad Kashmir.'

'So, you don't identify as an Indian? After everything the government has done for you?' Arjun snapped, his anger now directed at the driver.

'The government has done nothing for us; in fact, because of the government and the army, we'd rather be free. Azad Kashmir,' the driver said calmly.

Pooja stepped in. 'Okay, let's just stop talking, please.'

Arjun remained silent for the rest of the ride, but kept shooting furious looks at the driver.

When they reached their apartment, an unexpected wave of hostility greeted them. Fliers were strewn all over the pavement and stuck to their mailbox and door. ENP—the hard-line nationalist party—had plastered caricatures and messages warning immigrants to go back. One flier had a pig and a cow. Pooja didn't need help interpreting the metaphor. 'Well, this is a great welcome,' Arjun grunted.

They stepped inside, surveying the apartment, when the doorbell rang. An elderly woman stood outside, wicker basket in hand.

'Hello, dears; I'm your neighbour—Mrs Wilson. I thought I'd welcome you with some laddus I made today.'

'Oh, that's so sweet of you, Mrs Wilson; please come in. I'm Pooja, and this is my husband, Arjun.'

'I saw those fliers and didn't want your first day here to be ruined.'

Mrs Wilson noticed Pooja staring at the box of laddus and knew what she was thinking. 'I left India when I was 23—after my marriage,' she explained, 'but my homeland never left me. I'm 88 now. My family—my parents and sisters—lived there.'

'What happened to them?'

'My parents died years ago. One of my sisters settled in Australia and has a family there. Another sister and her husband passed away a decade ago. Their daughter is a doctor in the States now.'

And that was how Pooja had met Mrs Wilson. Through all her lows and highs in the UK, Mrs Wilson had been her constant source of joy and wisdom. As excited as she would get about gulab jamun and other Indian dishes, she was even more passionate about Indian culture and philosophy.

'You must read history, dear,' Mrs Wilson had once told Pooja while dusting off a hardcover book. 'If there's any real treasure in this world, it's right there—in your culture's history. Countless people have sought salvation, knowledge and purpose in it. Steve Jobs. The Beatles. Wilfred Bion.'

'Who's Bion?'

'A philosopher, like Sigmund Freud. But Bion had a different view of the mind. Freud—everyone knows him—was a Jew raised by a Catholic nanny. But Bion was a Christian raised in India by a Hindu nanny, while his father worked for the British Raj.'

Mrs Wilson's eyes always sparkled when she spoke of ideas. 'When he finally understood the meaning of life, he defined it as a state of ultimate truth—what he called "O". Not many people know this, but I am convinced "O" came from "*Om*". A lot of people chant it every day without understanding its true meaning.'

'Arrogance is a great obstruction to wisdom; remember this, Pooja,' Mrs Wilson would often repeat. It was her favourite quote by Bion.

As Pooja sat in Dr Silva's car, she was reminded of their talks, their shared tea breaks, the way her wisdom would fall casually into conversation like petals from a tree. She really missed Mrs Wilson and the instant connection they had formed.

Mrs Wilson often spoke of her struggles with identity—a battle that began early, growing up in the Anglo-Indian community. Though she was raised in India and had absorbed the country's culture and values, her appearance and name set her apart. She was never truly accepted. People called her 'Angrez'—a slur wrapped in a smile, a reminder of her foreignness. The label haunted her, leaving her to wonder if it was a burden she would carry for the rest of her life. Despite her deep connection to her birthplace, she never felt entirely at home.

When the British left India, she was granted passage to England, but there too, she remained an outsider. 'Too British' for India. 'Too Indian' for Britain. That, she told Pooja, was the cruel legacy of imperialism—a fractured identity and a lifelong sense of displacement.

'I spent decades staring into mirrors and seeing a face that didn't match the values inside me,' she had said once. Still, she had found her purpose. She turned her pain into scholarship, eventually becoming a professor of cross-cultural studies and history.

Her work broke new ground, giving voice to those caught between cultures. She spoke at conferences, wrote widely debated papers and mentored students who had also grown up asking, 'Where do I belong?'

Despite the trauma she carried, Mrs Wilson approached the world with gentleness and nuance. Her life became a testimony: that we are more than our categories. That identity is fluid, complex and sacred.

It was only then that Pooja realized just how much of her worldview had been shaped by the conversations she'd had with Mrs Wilson. Listening to her had taught Pooja to approach human experiences with nuance, humility and an open mind—to leave assumptions at the door, to choose empathy over reductionism. And now, as she looked at the quiet child sitting next to her in the car, the lesson had never felt more alive.

'Pooja?' Ankit's voice broke her reverie. The car had stopped. They were parked in an underground garage, and Ankit was already stepping out.

As Ankit and Pooja started moving towards the lift, Dr Silva called out, 'Not that one—I have a private lift. This way,' as she walked down a side corridor.

Damn impressive, thought Pooja, as they stepped inside a penthouse; it was bigger than any she had ever seen.

On one wall hung a picture of Dr Silva with two women.

'Mrs Wilson?' Pooja whispered.

No one heard her. Dr Silva showed them around, opening cabinets and pointing out where the tea, sugar and towels were kept—in case they needed anything in her absence.

Then, with a quick thank you directed at Pooja and Ankit and a squeeze of Maya's hand, she left for the hospital again.

Pooja didn't get a chance to ask her about the photograph.

23

Humans: Truth-Telling Machines

Dr Silva's Office
Northbridge General Hospital

'Rachel, what's my rescheduled itinerary for the day?' Dr Silva asked as she entered her office, only to find her assistant missing. Instead, someone else was there.

'So, you're Dr Silva?' asked the patient from Room 206.

'What are you doing here?'

'Getting treatment. It wasn't my idea, though,' the woman replied steadily. 'I'm old and weak; I have lived my life. My body is not strong enough to go through the full regimen. It's Sanjay, my son, who persuaded me to come here.' She paused, her eyes searching Dr Silva's. 'Truth be told, I know I'm going to die soon. If not here, then maybe back home.'

'I mean, what are you doing in my office? Shouldn't you be in your room?' Dr Silva's voice betrayed her discomfort.

'I feel...ignored. Is it something about me that bothers you? Please, just tell me what it is.'

'Your family must be looking for you,' Dr Silva replied flatly.

'No. They're too busy looking for our maid. She's gone missing. Left when everyone was asleep. Fortunately, I was awake. These aching bones keep me up at all hours... So, where is she?' the old lady asked, her voice quiet but sharp.

'Somewhere safe.'

'Ever since we came here, I have felt something...off. I see it in your eyes. You have something against me... And my family. I may not be as educated, but I know people. I know how they think, what drives them, what repulses them...' She leaned forward slightly, voice firm now. 'You refused to treat me. You had my bed shifted to the farthest corner—away from your office window. I demand to know why.'

'You've never heard "no" in your life, have you?' Dr Silva's voice cracked, but not from weakness. 'Even now, in your rejection, you "demand" to know why. Guess what? It's time someone said no to you.'

Slamming the door behind her, she left the room.

Out in the open, far from the building, she spotted a solitary bench hidden behind a row of trees. Seething, she collapsed on to it and broke down.

Memories crashed over her like a tide—memories she'd held back for decades. For the first time in a very long time, Dr Silva let all her emotions out.

Time blurred. Hours may have passed, or just minutes. She did not know. Didn't care. But she did know what had to be done now. With trembling fingers, she rummaged through her bag, pulled out her mobile phone and started dialling.

The first call was to Dr Hawker, the dean. She explained everything—Maya, the morning decision, the patient's confrontation.

'This is bad,' Dr Hawker muttered into the phone. 'This is bad, Dr Silva. You know how much I trust your judgement, and we have always given you a free hand on most matters. But this... This is a sensitive issue; I wish you'd come to me first.'

There was a long sigh on the line. 'That old woman is sharp. I doubt she'll go to the police, not if what you say is true and there's something sketchy going on. But she *will* reach out to someone... Probably Dr Gray; he's the one who's friends with the family and recommended them in the first place. Dangerous man to cross.'

He paused again. 'Anyway, I'll handle him. Take the day off and go home. I'll keep you updated. I hope you'll do the same.'

She thanked him quietly and hung up. Second call: her lawyer. A more clinical conversation, all facts, dates and legal exposure. He took notes. Asked questions. Promised to begin preparing statements—just in case.

The final call: her home.

Ankit picked up.

'Ankit, it's me—Anita. Jaya Bhargava knows I took Maya this morning. I guess by now her whole family does. Stay tight; I'm on my way. I talked to Dr Hawker—he's on our side, for now.'

'Shit, how does she know?' Ankit asked.

'She was up early. Saw us.'

'Damn old people. And damn their advanced sleep phase syndrome,' Ankit sighed. 'I'll call Dr Jindal—have him meet us here, if you don't mind. His network could be useful.'

'Yeah, sure. Are you guys hungry? I can bring something.'

'No, Doctor. We already ate. Maya and Pooja are asleep in the guest room. I was trying to catch some sleep on the couch. We're all good.'

'All right, get some rest. I have keys—I'll let myself in. See you in a while.'

⸺∞⸺

24

Becoming

Dr Silva's Penthouse

Pooja woke up with a start. For a few minutes disoriented seconds, she couldn't remember where she was or what had woken her. Then it came to her—voices, coming from Dr Silva's living room. It must be her and Ankit.

As Pooja left the guest room and started walking towards them, her eyes fell on that picture again—the one with Mrs Wilson. Mrs Wilson looked younger in it—by at least 20 years. So different from the warm, grey-haired neighbour she remembered from her years in the UK.

What a small world, Pooja mused.

Dr Silva noticed her gaze and instinctively moved to stand beside her. Maybe it was the way Pooja looked at the portrait, or maybe it was just the unspoken human urge to finally say things aloud.

'I was born in India,' Dr Silva began softly, 'in a small village. Society there was divided—by birth, by caste, by tradition. We were at the bottom of that archaic pyramid, expected to serve the higher castes. In the land where people come seeking spiritual awakening, there is this other side happening in plain sight... And no one wants to talk about it. It's the status quo that hurts the most... I am sorry—I'm going off on a tangent.'

She paused, then continued, her voice more composed. 'My father died when I was just a toddler. A few years later, my mother passed too. The local women's council dropped me off at a government orphanage. It was...hell. If anyone ever wanted to paint a picture of what darkness in humanity looks like, they should visit a place like that.'

She took a deep breath. 'After a few years, I was adopted by a couple from the UK. My adoptive mother's family had stayed on in India after independence. She was a citizen, embraced the culture, ideas and philosophies—everything. But Indian society never accepted her due to her skin colour. She met a young American who was working in India as part of President Kennedy's Peace Corps agricultural initiative. They fell in love and married. Mrs Wilson was her sister—my aunt.'

Pooja was awestruck. Slowly, she began sharing her own connection to Mrs Wilson—how the woman had been a sweet and constant presence during her time in the UK.

'Where is your mother now?' Ankit asked Dr Silva.

'She passed away about 20 years ago,' she replied. 'After that, I retreated into solitude. There are too many things from my past that I don't want to remember, but also can't forget. Work became my only relief. A sweet deception. When we slow down, we are forced to look at ourselves.'

She gave a faint smile. 'I am sorry, my hospitality is

not great, but please—make yourselves at home.'

Her voice wavered, and for a moment, she looked like she might take it all back. Vulnerability didn't come easy. 'It's strange,' Pooja began, 'how we always thought you were perfect—so put together, like you came from some other universe. But when we start celebrating people, we often overlook, even forget, that they can have flaws, struggles, vulnerabilities. Thanks for sharing a part of your story. It has taken a weight off *my* shoulders, too! It helps me feel less alone in my own mess.'

'I have fulfilled all my dreams,' Dr Silva said quietly. 'People respect me. I stand tall in my field. But someone once told me that the biggest motivation for a child is to live the life their parents never had. That always resonated with me. And yes, I've done that. But now, I agree that I stand tall in society and at the pinnacle of my area of expertise, but when it all ends, I won't remember the treatments I mastered... I'll remember the mountains I was too afraid to climb. I have spent my life dreaming. I think now I want to finally awaken.'

༄

25

Omnipotence in Bursting Mode

Northbridge General Hospital

Dr Gray, Dr Jindal and Dr Silva looked on as a very agitated Sanjay Bhargava paced furiously across the room, trying to find the right words, seething with rage.

As soon as Dr Jindal had arrived at Dr Silva's place, he had taken Maya to the embassy and handed her over to the authorities. The Bhargavas were now being interrogated one by one and it looked like they could even face prison sentences if their fraudulent activities were exposed.

'I'm going to sue all three of you—and this entire hospital,' Sanjay finally exploded. 'First you kidnap our maid, then you go and report it. But you just wait—all her documents will check out. As soon as I get back her custody, I'll sue your sorry asses. You've no idea about the clout I carry. I'm a cabinet minister—way more powerful than your senators. In our city, there's an entire boulevard named after my father, with a statue of him in the chowk, the city centre. You just wait—I'll deal with all of you.'

'Get out, Sanjay. You're not in India,' a voice cut in. Jaya Bhargava entered the office, a nurse at her side.

'Maa, don't get involved. And at least don't take their side,' Sanjay snapped.

As his mother stared him down, he stormed out, throwing a glare at everyone in the room.

'Is your son usually this…angry, ma'am?' Dr Jindal asked.

'This isn't anger—it's fear,' Dr Silva interjected. 'Maybe for the first time in his life, he is in a place where his influence doesn't work. And where going to prison is actually a possibility.'

'And are we to assume you're here to reprimand us as well, ma'am?' Dr Gray followed up, since Mrs Bhargava had not responded to his first question.

'I'm not here to scold or argue. Rather, I'd like to use this opportunity for mutual benefit.'

'I don't follow,' Dr Gray said.

'This nurse just told me my test results are in. The standard regimen hasn't had any effect on my condition,' she replied flatly. 'I want you to consider assigning Dr Silva to my case. I don't want to live forever. But I intend to close some old business before the finitude of human life catches up to me.'

Dr Gray's face fell. He knew, as everyone did, that Dr Silva would never agree to take Jaya Bhargava on as a patient.

'I'll think about it,' Dr Silva spoke up, her voice composed. 'I'll inform everyone of my decision by the end of the week. Till then, let's stick with the current regimen and observe for any changes.'

The room went silent, stunned.

Mrs Bhargava left, clearly satisfied with the outcome.

As the door clicked shut behind her, Dr Gray turned to Dr Silva, astonished. 'Well, that was...unexpected. You're not exactly known for changing your decisions. What happened?'

'Nothing. My actions brought unnecessary trouble to the hospital, and to you. It's the least I could do.'

With that, Dr Silva walked out of the Director's Office and went to her own.

She sat at her desk and covered her face with both hands. Her heart pounded, sweat clinging to her skin. Memories she had long buried began clawing their way back to the surface.

She had recognized the old woman the moment she'd seen her. But her mind had refused to believe it—until she saw the name printed on the file: Mrs Jaya Bhargava.

The mere sight of her was unbearable. Anita Silva had always put her work ethics above all else. No matter the patient, no matter the situation. But this one—this one had broken something inside her. This was the one patient she couldn't face.

Her phone rang, breaking through her spiral.

'Rachel?' she answered, her voice uneven.

'Doctor, are you done with the meeting?'

'Yes, I'm free now. What's going on?'

'I have good news. Shukla's office called. They've located the place where the bangles were manufactured. It's a small facility run by local craftsmen—generations of bangle-makers, apparently.'

'This is great news,' Dr Silva replied, slowly composing herself. 'Cancel my appointments for tomorrow afternoon and schedule the call.'

'Will do, Doctor. One more thing—we need to finalize your sari for the engagement. We have got less than two weeks left and still need to sort your attire and a gift for the couple.'

Much to everyone's delight, Ankit and Pooja had decided to get engaged.

'Rachel, I do not have the time or will to dwell upon fabrics and mementos. It's your department—choose whatever you think is appropriate. Isn't it in your job description anyway to make my life easier?'

'Not yet, Doctor. Not yet.'

'All right, from now on, consider it added to your job description—selecting attire and gifts.' Silva paused. 'Now that we've gotten this out of the way, listen to me carefully. I want Jaya Bhargava added to my schedule starting Monday. Also, I want all her files on my desk as soon as possible.'

'All right, Doctor. Anything else?'

'No, that'll be it.' Then—

'Wait, Rachel! Remember that magnificent dinner set I keep in the closet? The orange one?'

'The one I keep eyeing? Yes, Doctor, I remember. Is it my bonus for the expanded job description?'

'You wish. No. Get it cleaned and packed. I want to give it to Pooja. That dinner set was a gift from my aunt, who was also close to Pooja during her stay in the EU.

I'm sure she will like it.'

Then, summoning a rare courage, Dr Silva added, 'Rachel, I have been meaning to ask you this for quite some time... Are you free this weekend? Let's go grab some coffee.'

Rachel was shocked. It had never happened before. There was complete silence on the other end of the phone.

Dr Silva hurried on, 'Thank you for everything. Behind all the glitzy aura, you are the pivot that keeps me going—and that's not what I am thanking you for. It's for tolerating my rudeness, abruptness, snapping and entitlement. I learn from you every day, Rachel. And I am truly thankful to have you.'

Without waiting for Rachel's reply, Dr Silva hung up the call.

Rachel was not surprised—not really. She knew what kind of person Dr Silva was beneath that tough exterior. But hearing those words—out loud—was music to her ears. No one else got $5,000 gift cards for holidays. Silva's actions had always spoken louder than words. But Rachel had yearned to hear them forever. And the wait was worth it.

26

The Right to Make Mistakes

Dr Jindal's House

'Appear weak when you're strong and strong when you're weak. What do you think this one means, Dr Jindal?' Ankit asked, cradling his copy of *The Art of War* in his lap.

Spending Sunday afternoons at the Jindals'—lazing around with lemonade or homemade squash and a book in hand—had now become a ritual for him, especially after his proposal to Pooja. With an engagement party to plan, Dr Jindal's house had become the headquarters for all the preparations.

'Ravi has never read that book in his life; I can vouch for that. As to why you are reading a book on warfare, I haven't the faintest idea. Shouldn't you be reading some romantic novella, Ankit? You're getting engaged in a couple of weeks. I'd suggest ditching Mr Sun Tzu and picking up Nicholas Sparks or, maybe, Margaret Mitchell; even John Green, perhaps,' Mrs Jindal interjected.

'All the more reason to read about warfare, my dear. Wouldn't you agree that married life is a lifelong war, with new battles being fought every day?' Dr Jindal asked his wife, grinning. Then he turned to Ankit, 'As for your quote, I can only make an educated—let's discuss it when Mrs Jindal is out of earshot. I don't want to get into trouble.'

Ankit let out a snort of laughter as Mrs Jindal mockingly tapped her husband on the head.

'You mean any *more* trouble?' Ankit smirked. 'Also, it reminds me—I came over to talk about something important. Dr Jindal, while I appreciate your offer, I certainly cannot accept it. It would be too much trouble for you.'

The Jindals had offered their country house as the venue for the engagement party. A two-hour drive from the city, it boasted a huge hall, an even bigger lawn and a surreal countryside view.

Ankit and Pooja, after much discussion, had decided to politely decline the offer. As much as they loved the idea, they felt it was a lot to ask of the Jindals, who had already done so much for them.

'No, I'm not hearing a word about it, Ankit,' Mrs Jindal spoke up. 'The party will be hosted there, and that is final. If Pooja is the one filling your head with such nonsense, don't worry—I'll handle her. You just focus on your warfare lessons... And your guest list. I need numbers for the caterer.'

'We're still working on it. Which reminds me—I need another favour from you, Doctor.'

'What is it?'

'Pooja's parents... They aren't coming to the engagement. They're still not over the fact that she divorced her "perfect" husband. And they are even more disappointed that she is marrying another doctor—one who's neither rich nor good-looking like the first. As much as Pooja claims to be unaffected, I know it's bothering her; she's hurt. So I had this idea.

'Dr Silva has an aunt—Mrs Wilson. She lives in the UK and was like a motherly figure to Pooja when she was there. I was thinking of inviting her as a surprise. I can't ask Pooja for her contact details. That leaves us with Dr Silva. Since you have known her longer, could you ask her when you see her next?'

'Absolutely! It's a good idea. Do you want me to talk to Pooja's parents as well? Maybe I'll be able to convince them.'

'No, I have taken that on myself; I'll try and win them over. I may not live up to the standards they've set, but I love their daughter—and they need to see that.'

'All the best, son, in your noble endeavour,' Mrs Jindal said warmly. 'Dr Jindal also took it upon himself to woo my parents… And failed spectacularly. It was only when his elder brother interjected that this match became a possibility,' she added, chuckling.

'Oh yes, it was a disaster,' Dr Jindal groaned. 'I was told that Mr Dayal—my father-in-law—enjoyed wine. So, to impress him, I brought along a fine bottle of Candour Rosé. Turned out, it was the junior Mr Dayal—Mrs Jindal's brother—who enjoyed the wine. Her father was strictly against alcohol. The moment I handed him the bottle, I was doomed.

'And then for her mother, I brought a bouquet of seasonal flowers—only to learn she had a severe pollen allergy. I tell you, Ankit, I ran out of there so fast, because if I hadn't, they would have thrown me out. I returned the next day with my elder brother, who stepped in and saved the day. We got married thanks to him.'

'That is the most hilarious thing I've heard in a long time!' Ankit said between roars of laughter, the book slipping from his lap as he imagined the scene.

27

Redemption

Oncology Department
Northbridge General Hospital

Dr Silva was on her morning rounds, checking on patients one by one—asking how they were feeling, assessing their charts and trying to determine whether their regimen was working.

When she reached Mrs Bhargava, she avoided eye contact and carried on with her usual efficiency—checking vitals, scanning reports and asking how she was feeling.

'Foolish,' came the unexpected reply.

'Sorry, what?' Dr Silva blinked.

'You asked me how I'm feeling, Doctor; I'm feeling really foolish,' Mrs Bhargava repeated flatly.

'Care to elaborate, please?'

'I think it is you who should elaborate. I asked you before, and you lied to my face. I still don't understand why you refused to treat me. We travelled across countries, spent thousands just to get under your care, and you rejected me without explanation.'

Her voice was raspy but loud enough to carry down

the entire wing, the sound echoing off the thin walls that offered little privacy. In a hospital like this—old and with rooms not quite sealed from each other—everything could be heard. Nobody had ever seen anyone speak to Dr Silva like this.

Dr Silva swallowed hard. 'You are assuming things, ma'am; It was nothing that.'

'Exactly why I feel foolish. You made me believe everything was normal. But you are hiding something. I want to know why you denied me treatment before—and why, suddenly you have had a change of heart.' Her tone had sharpened, each word laced with anger.

Dr Silva fought to stay composed. 'I do not understand what you're trying to say. And please—this tone is unacceptable.'

Emotions surged beneath the surface, but she kept her face unreadable. 'I have never faced such rejection in my life,' Mrs Bhargava replied, her voice trembling. 'It's killing me more than the cancer is. It's a...strange feeling.'

After years of living a feudal, privileged life, always getting her way, Silva's silent rejection had unearthed something deeper than offence. It hurt. It unsettled her.

She pressed on. 'Don't get me wrong, I am not pleading for your care. I'm just trying to explain this discomfort—this new feeling you've made me experience.'

'Please, let me do my work,' Silva replied, not wanting the conversation to continue any further.

But Mrs Bhargava couldn't stop, even as she struggled to find the right words. 'You are missing my point; I feel... Something new... Fresh! Like a mix of joy and sadness. Euphoria, maybe. But also, the sight of your face brings a deep, aching pain.'

'Helplessness?' Dr Silva indulged the old woman.

'No, not exactly!'

There was a pause. Then Dr Silva spoke up, slowly and deliberately. 'One of my acquaintances—she's a genius—had a similar experience. Top of her class, brilliant in the arts, unbeatable at sports... She went on to earn an MBA, became a CEO and married the perfect man. But she couldn't have children. For years, she tried everything, but nothing worked. She got very depressed and sought therapy.

'The psychoanalyst told her it was the best thing that could ever happen to her. She got furious, thinking he was mocking her, making fun of her misery. He said, "You have achieved everything through effort, money and connection. But this—this you can't control. It's just not in your hands. And it's teaching you something nothing else could."

'I think...that experience made her humble,' Dr Silva concluded. She hoped Mrs Bhargava would find something similar in her pain.

Mrs Bhargava said nothing. Her lips quivered as tears welled up in her eyes. She sat silently, trying to process the unfamiliar emotion that had taken root—something beyond words, raw and real.

28

Integrity or Despair

Oncology Department
Northbridge General Hospital

Dr Silva had just reached her office when an urgent page came through. The patient in Room 206 had collapsed in the bathroom and she was to attend to her immediately. Dr Silva set off towards the ward, escorted by her team.

By the time they arrived, Mrs Bhargava was in a stable condition, following CPR. Dr Silva stayed in the room longer than she usually did, quietly reviewing the reports while also watching the old lady breathe, as if the rhythm might tell her something no chart could.

Mrs Bhargava eventually stirred. Spotting Dr Silva seated beside her, she gave a faint smile. 'Dr Silva, I can see in your eyes—you are troubled by me.'

Caught off guard, Dr Silva looked momentarily startled before she schooled her expression. 'I'm just doing my job,' she replied curtly.

'Will you be abandoning me again, like before?' she asked.

Dr Silva scoffed. 'Do you understand what that word means? Do you even know what you are saying? Do you know what neglect is? You're an ignorant and ruthless woman. You don't get to talk to me like that.'

Tears stung her eyes as her voice cracked. Without another word, she bolted from the room, left the hospital and drove home—barely seeing the road as the past came crashing back.

She had once been the blue-eyed girl of her family. Her parents had moved to a new city to work for an upper-caste household, disguising their background just to survive. But one day, the truth slipped through the cracks—a postcard from their village exposed their caste.

Everything changed.

The family head had ordered them to vacate the bungalow premises immediately. The humiliation on her parents' faces—tears, helplessness—had etched itself into her soul. And then—the purifying ritual. House staff dusting and scrubbing the room they had lived in, as if her family had contaminated it.

That memory scarred her.

She remembered walking out of that grand mansion with her parents, only to glance up at the window and see a young Jaya Bhargava watching them silently, like a queen overseeing the fallen.

Her life changed drastically after that.

Her father passed away soon after, and her mother fell ill—severe abdominal pain with recurrent vomiting. They waited endlessly at the government clinic, only to be turned away. Eventually, they took her to a private hospital that demanded a large sum up front—money they didn't have. They were told that it was a serious problem that needed surgery. She later learnt it was a treatable condition, one that could've been fixed for less than 30 cents.

After her mother passed away, she lived in a government shelter until she was adopted and moved to the United States. She would never forget the day Mrs Silva and Mrs Wilson came to pick her up, and she had to say goodbye to everything she had ever known.

29

The Last Sacrifice

Northbridge General Hospital

Mrs Bhargava in Room 206 was more than just another patient. For Dr Silva, she was a ghost from a buried past—a living reminder of betrayal, shame and sorrow she had spent a lifetime trying to forget.

Fragments of memory drifted through Silva's mind like shards of broken glass. Some things were impossible to forget, yet the face of the man at the centre of it all remained elusive—blurred by years of sorrow and distance. What she did remember clearly was the feel of smooth marbles in her tiny hands, and the rustling leaves of the ancient banyan tree, its sprawling branches casting intricate patterns on the worn, sun-bleached structures around her. The mansion had been a labyrinth of rooms and verandas, alive with the hum of rituals. The late afternoon breeze would gently stir the curtains and, for a fleeting moment, it felt like life itself was celebrating.

Even as a child, she had sensed a divide. From her dim, cramped quarters, she would gaze longingly towards the brighter side of the house, where warmth and laughter lingered. Her parents had drawn an invisible line red line—one she was forbidden to cross. On the other side was a world that radiated privilege and belonging, while she remained cloaked in quiet alienation and unspoken deprivation. She had always been the 'other', and her young heart had borne the weight of that knowledge.

The ache sat like a stone on her chest, pulling her back into the present. Dr Silva blinked, shaking herself free from the past. The flashback faded, and she was once again in Jaya's hospital room, standing amid sterile machines and quiet beeps.

Each day, Dr Silva felt slipping deeper into the shadows of her own mind. Long-buried memories clawed their way to the surface, threatening to consume her once again. In those moments of vulnerability, a darker voice whispered to her—tempting her to embrace the bitterness that had long simmered beneath her polished exterior. She ignored it. She adjusted Mrs Bhargava's medication regimen and continued the treatment.

Within a week, Jaya Bhargava began responding to Silva's unique off-label combination therapy. With that, her family began preparing for their return home.

∞

30

The Silence between Words

It had been a couple of weeks since Mrs Bhargava had begun responding well to the treatment. She had been discharged and was scheduled to return to India the following day. With a sigh of relief, Dr Silva drove home from the hospital after a night shift—but she stopped short as she approached a school.

It was the start of the new academic year. Children were being dropped off for their first day, some experiencing the anxiety of separation for the very first time. Parents stood around, teary-eyed and hesitant, reluctant to leave. Dr Silva watched them silently as tears welled up in her own eyes. The sight of such vulnerable goodbyes stirred something deep within her.

Once home, she poured herself a cup of coffee and stood by the window, watching the world drift by in slow motion.

The doorbell rang.

One of the hospital chauffeurs stood outside, with Jaya Bhargava beside him.

'I'm sorry, Doctor,' the chauffeur said. 'She wanted to meet you before flying home. I was asked to bring her here by Dr Gray.'

Jaya stepped inside slowly. Without waiting for an invitation, she looked at Silva and asked softly, 'Have you forgiven me?'

Silva nodded towards the couch in her living room, gesturing for her to sit.

As they settled down, Dr Silva said, 'I don't take things to heart. Whatever happened between us—the words we exchanged—perhaps they were unnecessary... I usually don't meet people at home, but since you are here, I wish you good luck and good health.'

Mrs Bhargava glanced around the room—and her eyes froze on a photo frame hanging on the wall. It held a picture of a much younger Silva, from the time she was adopted out of foster care. Jaya stood abruptly, walked closer to the frame and stared in disbelief.

Dr Silva noticed her behaviour and frowned, her jaw tightening.

'I knew it,' Mrs Bhargava whispered. 'I felt it the moment I saw you. We met long before your hospital ever came into my life.'

She turned to Dr Silva. 'I loved you as my own child; my heart can't be wrong about recognizing you,' she said.

Dr Silva's face turned pale, her eyes wide with shock. 'What are you talking about?' she asked, though deep down, she already knew.

'I began searching for you when I finally gathered the courage. I was weak back then—dependent, naïve. After Raj, my elder son, died, I slipped into depression. I repented every day for what I allowed to happen to you and your family,' Mrs Bhargava replied, her voice trembling.

Dr Silva closed her eyes. A tear slipped down her cheek.

'You were like my first child,' Jaya continued. 'I was newly married, idealistic—I thought everyone would be helpful and kind. You brought joy into my life. We went for walks, attended every event in town, visited the temple and the library. I bought you every book you wanted to read. People used to ask if you were my child...

'The day you were thrown out of the house, it felt like someone had placed a mountain on my chest. I should have spoken up. But I was terrified—of my husband, of my in-laws, of society. I had no voice then. How could I have been so weak?' she finished, her voice cracking.

After a moment, Dr Silva asked, 'What happened to Raj?'

'He died after suffering a head injury during a bar fight. He needed a blood transfusion. Ironically, it was our driver who had the matching blood type and was ready to help. But he was not "good enough". After his death, we finally realized...we had created a monster. He was worse than the generations before him. We enabled that.

'Vikram, my husband, had a stroke soon after and lost the elections. Although he is still a character, he has changed. He's softer now...more reflective. He's cried more in the last decade than I ever thought possible. I think losing Raj made him human.'

Jaya's voice softened further. 'He sees the pain he caused others now. And he blames himself. I've seen him looking at your photos—we still have a few from those days. He never says anything, but in his eyes... I see regret. And I see shame. You brought a joy into our home that never returned.'

Dr Silva exhaled slowly, the weight of the past pressing heavily on her chest. 'I think, when we reach the end of our lives, we finally begin to understand what we truly earned... And what we are leaving behind,' she replied quietly.

'I want to say I am sorry, Dr Silva. I am so proud of you! You've become someone remarkable. You deserve more than an apology. We are so ashamed—truly embarrassed by how we treated you.'

Silva looked away. 'I am not proud of myself,' she whispered. 'I have been so angry...caught in self-pity and bitterness. Conflicted for years.'

Mrs Bhargava nodded, her voice growing firmer. 'At some point, we all need meaning and purpose in our lives. A reason to keep going. We lost that. Our lives became like blocks of wood—shapeless, purposeless. When we should have spoken up, we stayed silent. And this...this is the cost of silence. We all knew it was wrong.'

∽∞∽

A few months later, Dr Silva received a phone call at four in the morning. As she listened to the voice on the other end, her expression went blank. It was Vikram.

'She's gone,' he said softly. Jaya had passed away.

Dr Silva hung up and sat still for some time. The silence in the room was deafening. It felt as though a weight she had carried all these years had suddenly lifted.

The sensation was strange—unfamiliar. She stared

blankly at the wall for a moment, then looked down at her hands. They were relaxed, unclenched. Even the soft gust of air from the ceiling vent brushed against her skin with an awareness she hadn't felt in years.

Her senses, usually dulled by routine and memory, were now fully awake. For the first time in a long while, she wasn't just existing inside her mind—she was present.

After several moments of calm, her eyes began scanning the room, searching for something. Teary-eyed, she finally found it—on her nightstand. The cold, hard brass plate.

It was dusty, but she knew what it said by heart. Her vision blurred as she read the inscription—words she had memorized long ago:

'I swear by Apollo Physician and Asclepius and Hygieia and Panacea and all the gods and goddesses, making them my witnesses, that I will fulfil according to my ability and judgement this oath and this covenant…'

As she stared at the Oath of Hippocrates, a fleeting thought crossed her mind: had her off-label regimen hastened Jaya's death? The thought vanished as quickly as it had appeared. But in some quiet, unexplored corner of her mind, there was a cold, subtle stirring. A chilling recognition.

Not guilt—at least, not entirely. Something murkier.

A sinister satisfaction, perhaps. The kind one doesn't admit, even to oneself.

The next morning, Dr Silva landed in India. A chauffeur sent by the Bhargava family waited at the airport, holding a small placard with her name. She got into the car silently, the engine humming as it moved through the city's narrow streets towards the cremation ground.

Upon arrival, she stepped out into the warm, dusty air. Jaya's body lay wrapped in white cloth, placed upon the wooden pyre. There was no sound except the crackling of firewood being arranged and the murmurs of ritual.

Dr Silva's eyes drifted towards a tall stone pillar standing near the cremation site. On it was an inscription in an unfamiliar script. She stood still, staring at it, drawn to its quiet solemnity. Curiosity pulled at her. Reaching into her coat pocket, she took out her phone, unlocked it and did a quick image search.

Within seconds, the results flooded her screen. She clicked on one that explained the term in detail—Antyeṣṭi (Sanskrit: अन्त्येष्टि): the final sacrament in Hindu tradition. The rites and ceremonies of funeral rituals. The ultimate farewell to the departed soul. The last sacrifice.

Silva looked back at Jaya's body on the pyre. In that moment, the word transformed in her mind. Antyeṣṭi was no longer just a ritual.

It became a symbol—of closure.

She remained there for a long time, eyes fixed on the inscription, the flames crackling behind her, memories swirling quietly in the smoke.

Epilogue

After the cremation was over, Dr Silva bid farewell to the Bhargavas and left for the place her heart had longed to return to. She took a cab and arrived at the orphanage where she had spent her childhood before being adopted at the age of 11.

She paused at the gate, took a deep breath, and stepped inside. The echoes of her footsteps reverberated through the corridors—familiar, yet changed. Each step took her deeper into the fragmented remains of her past.

Dr Silva's heart raced as she navigated the halls, haunted by the laughter of children who had once shared this space with her. The caretaker, a soft-spoken woman with kind eyes, led her to the room that held the echoes of her two-year stay—two years without anyone to call family.

As the door creaked open, Dr Silva felt herself transported to a time when hope still flickered in her eyes—a hope to leave, to belong, to be loved.

The dim light filtered through the windows, casting a soft glow on the worn-out toys and faded drawings that still clung to the walls. Her eyes welled with a bittersweet mix of nostalgia and tenderness. She ran her fingers along the drawings—remnants of a childhood she had spent years trying to forget.

The caretaker quietly stepped away, giving Dr Silva the space she needed.

As the floodgates of emotion opened, a strange peace settled over her. This place, once a symbol of loss and abandonment, was now a cradle of her resilience. She wasn't here to relive the past—she was here to reshape a future. She had come to adopt a child from the very orphanage that had shaped her own destiny.

The caretaker gently ushered her into the office and introduced her to the official in charge. After a brief exchange, he looked at her with measured curiosity.

'Dr Silva, we appreciate your visit. It's not every day that former residents return,' he said.

'Thank you. It's been a journey down memory lane, to say the least,' she replied.

'I can imagine. Is there something specific you're looking for?'

'An unexplained longing, perhaps,' she said softly. 'But also, I've come with a purpose. I want to adopt a girl from here.'

The official straightened slightly in his chair. 'That's commendable. We can begin discussing the necessary documents. You could bring your husband on your next visit, and then—'

'There is no husband,' Dr Silva interrupted, her tone curt. 'There's no would-be father.'

He blinked, caught off guard. 'You're not married, Dr Silva?'

She gave a firm nod.

He hesitated, adjusting his glasses. 'Our procedures

usually favour traditional family structures. Even though the law permits single-parent adoptions, I must tell you—it's not an easy path.'

'I understand,' she said simply, her expression unchanged.

'It's not about doubting your capability,' he added quickly. 'But societal norms...they can be rigid. Single-parent adoptions often face greater scrutiny.'

Dr Silva offered no further response. Her silence—calm, unflinching—spoke louder than any argument. It was her way. She had learnt that silence could be sharper than confrontation.

The official seemed to realize something in that moment. Perhaps it was her composure. Perhaps it was the way his own words, spoken aloud, suddenly sounded small.

'Your dedication is evident, Dr Silva,' he said at last. 'There will be legal procedures, paperwork, home assessments...'

'I'm ready for whatever it takes,' she said. 'I've faced challenges before. This is no different.'

He gave a faint smile, one that seemed to carry a flicker of respect. 'Very well. Let's begin the process. Perhaps together, we can change a few minds.'

What followed was a maze—legal systems in two countries, interviews, background checks, endless documentation. Each step was exhausting, but it was nothing Dr Silva hadn't endured before. In every meeting with lawyers, social workers, and officials, she held her ground—graceful, unwavering.

The day finally arrived when Dr Silva stood before the orphanage director, holding the legal documents that would unite her with a little girl who, like her, sought solace and love. The director's eyes gleamed with admiration as Dr Silva pledged to give the child a life that would transcend the scars of their shared past.

The caretaker asked, 'You don't have to—but would you like to give her a special name? Maybe something like "little angel"?'

Caught completely off guard, Dr Silva paused. 'Hmm... Let me think,' she murmured, her mind racing. After a few moments of contemplation, she said, 'Aegle... no, no... Pan...Panacea. What do you think?'

The caretaker smiled. 'That sounds nice. I've never heard that name before. What does it mean?'

'It originates from a Greek story, about 2,400 years ago,' Dr Silva began. 'A renowned healer named Asclepius was said to possess a panacea—a cure for everything. He even dared to heal those destined to die. But for this defiance, Zeus, the king of gods, struck him down with a thunderbolt. Still, Asclepius's memory lived on in temples where people sought healing. The idea of a panacea—a cure-all—may be a fleeting dream, but the spirit of Asclepius endures. A symbol of compassion and resilience in the timeless quest for wellness.'

The caretaker nodded thoughtfully. 'Interesting... Probably a reminder that death is the ultimate truth and cannot be evaded. No wonder Asclepius had to be silenced—he could've made humans immortal. What a story—and what an incredible name. What else can be said?' He smiled. 'Have a safe journey.'

With the legalities behind her, Dr Silva prepared to bring the child home to the United States. The flight back was more than a physical journey; it marked the emotional distance she had travelled from the lonely, guarded person she once was.

As the plane landed, Dr Silva held the hand of little Panacea. The child bore the soft features of Indian heritage—dark, cascading hair, a cherubic face, and almond-shaped eyes that shimmered with curiosity and warmth. The story had come full circle.

Dr Silva boarded the plane with quiet determination, her steps deliberate as she clutched her bag tightly. Once the cabin lights dimmed, signalling the beginning of their journey, she leaned back in her seat. Her fingers trembled slightly as they slipped into her bag. Carefully, she retrieved a small, delicately wrapped packet.

She glanced at the young girl beside her—a girl with a smile so open and bright it could light up even the darkest corners of grief. Dr Silva placed the packet gently on Panacea's lap.

Panacea, wide-eyed and filled with excitement, began to unwrap the delicate layers with care. As she peeled away the final wrapping to reveal an ornate box, her breath caught. Slowly, she lifted the lid—and her eyes widened at the sight inside: a set of bangles, intricate and radiant, adorned with ancient stones that seemed to whisper of civilizations long gone. The colours shimmered in the dim cabin light, dancing like tiny rainbows—each flicker a story of heritage, love and survival.

Panacea's face lit up with joy, her smile stretching from ear to ear. She gently traced the edges of the bangles, her fingers trembling slightly with wonder. The look in her eyes was pure, unrestrained delight—a moment of being truly seen, truly loved.

Dr Silva watched her in silence, her heart swelling with a kind of relief she hadn't known she needed. She didn't speak, but her gaze said everything: *I love you.* And *I want you to live this life.*

As Panacea giggled and slipped the bangles onto her slender wrists, Dr Silva felt a wave of emotion rise within her. A single tear traced down her cheek, then another, as she turned to stare out the window at the endless sky beyond. The moment was sweet, but it was also heavy.

The child's joy stirred memories—of the life Dr Silva had lost, of the mistakes she had made, of the burdens she had carried alone for too long. And yet...something inside her shifted. In the warmth of Panacea's laughter, in her bright, unburdened eyes, Dr Silva found something close to closure.

It was as though, for the first time, she could truly envision a future—a path forward built not on forgetting the past, but on honouring it. A path paved with humility, healing, and love.

As the plane soared through the clouds, Dr Silva closed her eyes and let the weight of the moment wash over her. For the first time in what felt like forever, she allowed herself to hope—

For Panacea.

For herself.

For the life they would build together.

Hand in hand, they faced the future. Two stories intertwined—one healing the other, and in doing so, becoming whole again.

∞

Acknowledgements

I am profoundly grateful to my late grandfather, Shrinivas Gupta, whose quiet wisdom and steady presence laid the earliest foundation for my intellectual and personal growth. In a world that often rewards compliance and punishes doubt, he fostered an environment where free thinking was not just allowed but actively encouraged. He believed, as I have come to believe, that the freedom to think is the first great step towards the freedom to speak.

He stood as a gentle guardian of my developing mind, shielding me from the weight of dogma and the pressures of conformity. Never once did he impose value judgements on my curiosities or ideas; instead, he encouraged me to question what others might have deemed unquestionable, to sit with uncertainty and to honour the process of becoming.

His influence resonates throughout this book, not through grand declarations or inherited ideologies, but through the quiet yet powerful principle that true learning begins where imposed certainty ends. It is to him I owe the courage to write, the freedom to explore and the humility to keep asking.